SURVIVING SPRING

BREAK WITH RYAN

RUPERT

By

P.S.Malcolm

to tyler, who taught me how a heart breaks.

CONTENTS

PROLOGUE..11

CHAPTER ONE...15

CHAPTER TWO..34

CHAPTER THREE...64

CHAPTER FOUR...74

CHAPTER FIVE...100

CHAPTER SIX...118

CHAPTER SEVEN..138

CHAPTER EIGHT...149

CHAPTER NINE...164

CHAPTER TEN..170

CHAPTER ELEVEN..193

CHAPTER TWELVE..210

CHAPTER THIRTEEN...231

CHAPTER FOURTEEN..252

CHAPTER FIFTEEN...269

CHAPTER SIXTEEN...287

CHAPTER SEVENTEEN..301

CHAPTER EIGHTEEN...310

CHAPTER NINETEEN..321

CHAPTER TWENTY...335

CHAPTER TWENTY-ONE..345

CHAPTER TWENTY-TWO..362

CHAPTER TWENTY-THREE.......................................375

CHAPTER TWENTY-FOUR..382

EPILOGUE..388

ACKNOWLEDGEMENTS...399

ABOUT THE AUTHOR...401

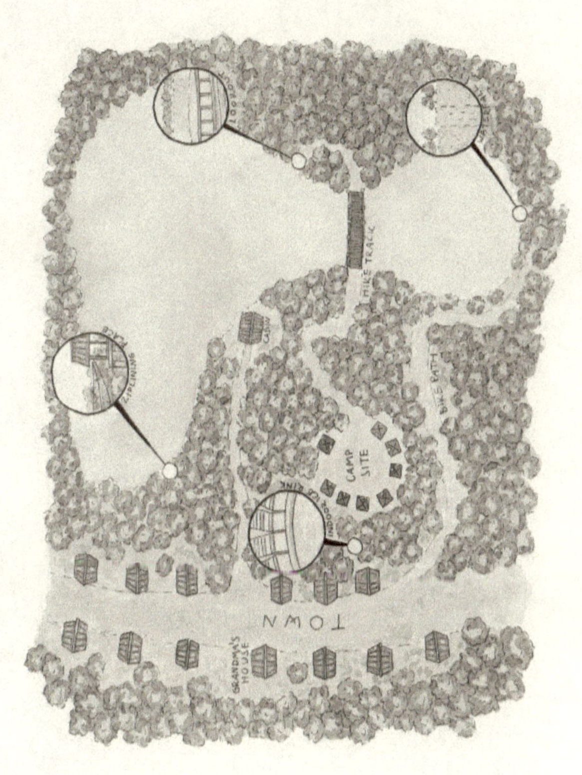

TOWN
HIKE TRACK
BIKE PATH
CAMP SITE
CABIN
ZIPLINING
GRANDMA'S HOUSE
INDOOR ICE RINK

PROLOGUE

Ryan's POV

"**I**'m hungry!" Aubany whined, like the little brat she was. Trailing behind her parents as they hiked over a decaying, fallen log, she looked positively miserable. The sight filled me with the richest delight.

"Seriously? You ate, like, *two hours* ago," I replied. The leaves under my feet crunched as I walked. "If you eat any more, you'll get all fat! Then you'll look like a balloon!"

Aubany shot me a dirty glare before whipping her head towards her mom—her red hair flying in the process. She stomped her foot.

"*Mom!* Ryan's being mean again!"

"Oh, for pity's sake, you two, would you cut it *out?"* Mrs. Winters scolded, looking at the two of us over her shoulder. She wore a huge backpack, and she had to peer down at us. "You've both done nothing but bicker for the entire trip!"

I saw Aubany grumble something under her breath and fold her arms over her chest, but it went unnoticed by Mrs. Winters.

Up ahead, my parents were taking photos with Mr. Winters on their brand-new *Nikon D80* camera. My mom spotted us coming up the hiking track and her eyes gleamed with excitement.

"Ryan! *Smile!*" she sang, pointing the lens my way. I grinned, and the shutter went off. She then went on to photograph Aubany, who was still pouting.

We'd been walking for what seemed like a million years. There hadn't been much to look at apart from trees, so when Dad announced that he could see something up ahead, my heart began to race with excitement.

"Look!" he said, pointing through the bristly pine trees. We all peered through the dense forestry, and made out what appeared to be a cabin. Dad took a step towards it, intending to go and check it out.

"Honey, that's someone's property," my mom scolded, pulling dad back. "We shouldn't pry."

The four adults continued onward, bickering about being *adventurous,* and I was about to follow them but I noticed Aubany sitting on a rock, pulling off her shoe. I couldn't help but roll my eyes.

"Come *on,* Aubany!" I said. Couldn't she wait until we got back to rest her feet?

"There's a rock in my shoe!" she protested, shaking her trainer up and down vigorously. I sighed, and decided to wait for her. The last thing we needed was for her to get lost. Grimacing, I looked around as I waited. My attention went back to the cabin, and to my surprise, I saw a girl standing in the view.

Staring at me.

The girl continued to watch us, and I got an uncomfortable feeling.

"Hurry up, Aubany, or I'm leaving without you," I said nervously, wanting to catch up to my parents. The girl's piercing stare was making me anxious.

"Just *wait!*" Aubany whined, tying her shoe laces. I anxiously kept an eye on the strange girl. She hadn't moved. Just continued to stare. What a *creep!*

"There!" Aubany announced, jumping up from the rock.

Finally! I grabbed her by the arm and tugged hard. Ignoring her protests, I dragged the both of us out of there, until we were a safe distance away, before resuming our normal pace.

Call me crazy, but something wasn't right about that girl, and I wasn't hanging around to find out what.

CHAPTER ONE

SPRING BREAK, BABY

Aubany's POV

Class could not go any slower. I tapped my pen on the desk irritably, unable to contain my energy. I'd been pumped since the beginning of the week, when it had finally hit me.

The holidays were here.

It had been a year and a bit since my last vacation to Nula Island. Although it hadn't been a dream vacation, it has still changed my life dramatically. Now, I had two new wonderful friends who keep in contact frequently through text and Skype. Savannah and Alex, who currently resided in Miami, were friends we had made on the island. But that wasn't the best part.

I had the most *amazing* boyfriend ever, and it was all because of that trip.

Beside me was my best friend since first grade, Melissa Carter, who shot me an annoyed look for tapping the pen repeatedly. I ceased the action, plastering a sheepish expression on my face. Unlike myself, she enjoyed English. In fact, I think she just enjoyed school in general. She wanted to become a lawyer one day, and she was aiming for Harvard University.

I was completely knackered after studying for finals all semester. Melissa, her boyfriend Lewis, and my boyfriend Ryan had all shared the same feeling. So, we'd decided to spend our half-term at Lewis' lake house cabin. None of us aside from Lewis had been there, but we'd heard it was really nice—situated out of town, it was dead peaceful and there were plenty of opportunities for bonfires and hanging out. It sounded perfect after a stressful semester.

All thoughts of an exciting, fun-filled trip vanished when my teacher, Mrs. Denners, began to proceed down the aisle. *That* could only mean one thing. I grimaced, wanting to bury my head in my hands.

"So, I want you to spend your break doing these tasks I've prepared for you," Mrs. Denners said, handing out a sheet of paper for each of us. I heard groans echo throughout the class, and even I suppressed a grunt of disapproval as a sheet was placed down in front of me. The entire span of the paper, from top to bottom, was packed with preparation research questions for next semester's unit.

The bell *finally* rang, and I grudgingly slipped the paper into my bag as everyone stood to leave. Not even a sheet of homework could permanently dull everyone's excitement for the holidays, and my classmates energetically filed out from the room, laughing and chatting excitedly. Melissa and I shuffled through the crowded halls to our lockers to gather what we needed before we headed home.

Melissa's locker was closer to the front entrance, so we went to mine first, which was all the way at the back of the school.

"Don't forget that we're leaving at seven--*sharp*--tomorrow," Melissa reminded me, as I shoved all the books I didn't need into the locker.

"Oh, you don't have to *remind* me. The idea has been plaguing me all week," I replied. As excited as I was for the trip, I didn't understand *why* we had to leave so early! "Blakesky isn't that far away. We'd still get there by nightfall if we left around lunchtime."

Melissa gave me a pointed look.

"You sound like you want to put the trip off," she stated, eying me curiously.

I sighed. "It's not that," I began. "I just like sleeping in, and this is the first time in *months* that I haven't had to work an early weekend shift," I admitted.

I'd been working as a barista for almost a year now, and I *loved* it— free coffee, chats with the regulars, and making the latte art look superb.. But it *did* mean I worked long weekend shifts. "It would be nice to be able to sleep in, you know, just *once.*"

Melissa rolled her eyes. "You can sleep in the car. We're got to leave early because Lewis wants to clean the place up when we arrive. It hasn't been visited in years. The last thing he'll want to do is clean everything if we get there late at night."

Well, I'd known it would be impossible to change her mind from the start, but at least I tried. With a woeful sigh, I shut my locker and turned to head towards the school entrance, only to run into a tall, built body of muscle. I looked up.

"Geez, someone's keen to see me," Ryan teased, as he steadied me. He grinned a cocky grin, and my expression of despair instantly melted into a smile as I wrapped my arms around him. I sank into his warmth and inhaled his familiar scent. A sense of security wrapped around me like a blanket.

Melissa coughed, which brought me back to my senses, and I reluctantly stepped away from Ryan. Melissa's gaze was one of steel as she eyed the two of us disapprovingly.

"You may need to see that this one gets out of bed on time tomorrow," Melissa told Ryan coldly. I would have shrunk away from such a gaze, but Ryan didn't seem fazed. In fact, he smirked at her.

"Don't worry. I'll turn the air conditioner up so it's freezing and pull the covers off of her, then lure her downstairs with coffee beans," he replied, and my eyes widened in protest.

"Don't you *dare!*" I said, the very thought of the situation making me shiver. "You may be my neighbour, but that doesn't mean you can break into my house in the early morning!"

"Why not? I've broken into your bedroom on countless occasions," he replied with a wink, and I flushed red. Melissa made a disgruntled noise and said,

"*Okay*--well, I'm going to head off now. I'll see you both tomorrow, *bright and early!*"

"Of course, *your majesty,*" I replied, with a hint of sarcasm, as she flipped her midnight black hair over her shoulder and headed through the thinning crowd.

Melissa still wasn't happy about my relationship with Ryan. As the person who had grown up with me over the years, she'd watched him bully me time and time again. And then, one summer, I disappear for six weeks, and we come back skipping and holding hands like the past seventeen years never happened. Melissa didn't approve, and she hasn't forgiven Ryan for his misdeeds yet. She almost didn't forgive me for letting him become such a prominent part of my life.

But the decision I made was mine alone to make, and that thought comforted me. I turned my attention back to Ryan, and just by looking at him I knew it was the best decision I've made so far.

"Did you get any homework to complete over the break?" I asked.

"Nope," he replied, his grin growing wider. My eyes narrowed with jealousy.

"You're so lucky. I'll probably have to do mine on the trip tomorrow, otherwise I just *know* I'll forget about it."

"Just don't do it. Be a *rebel,* Aubs," he teased, and I resisted the urge to swat at him.

"You're a bad influence," I scolded, as we began to walk through the halls.

"You're the *thrill seeker* in this relationship," he reminded me, and I knew it was a joke, not a taunt. Everything had flipped upside down compared to what it used to be between us. What was once in-tended to be harmful had become the foundation of our relationship.

And it was a foundation that was going to last...right?

When we got home, Ryan went next door to his house to greet his parents before coming over. My parents had suggested Ryan stay for dinner tonight, so Mom had gone out to get groceries and Dad was still at work. They hadn't been so shocked to hear we were dating— after all, I basically fed my Mom hints over the course of the vacation as to where our rela-tionship was heading. More importantly, they'd ac-cepted him, even after everything he'd done.

I think the ground breaker for my parents in par-ticular had been what Ryan had done for me on Nula Island. Putting himself in danger to protect me and helping me with my fears—it had been enough to prove he had only good intentions for me, which was all my parents had ever asked for when it came to the boys I dated. I knew they both adored Ryan.

Ryan came over soon enough, and we somehow ended up in the kitchen raiding the cupboard. After we'd found snacks, the two of us headed to the lounge room to play video games—one of Ryan's favourite past times that had somehow rubbed off on me. About four months into the relationship I'd ended up getting a PS4 and we'd both shared his stash of games until I developed my own taste.

Ryan and I settled on the couch and we continued playing a racing game he'd recommended a few weeks ago. I'd very quickly gotten through all of his shooting games which hadn't left a lot of options for multi-player games. What I really liked about this one is that we could focus on the game, but it was a lot easier to have a conversation with him about other things too. And I couldn't help what came out of my mouth next.

"Did you apply for that scholarship yet?" I asked. Lately, Ryan hadn't been too keen in discussing life outside of high school. Every time I bought it up he cringed away or changed the subject. But I wanted to make sure he was on the right track, and seeing as our futures were now *entwined,* I needed to know that he was on a path I could *also* walk on.

Just as I suspected, Ryan tensed up at the question.

"Not yet," he said quickly. I grimaced, my heart sinking as I glanced at him.

"You should do it soon," I said, trying to be gentle about my words. "You don't want to miss out, and I know it will help a lot."

"I know," he said. "I just don't know if it's the right thing to do yet."

"What do you mean?" I asked, sparing a quick glance at the TV screen. My car had driven off track and I was losing the race—but I didn't care.

"It's...I'm just thinking about things," he said. "Let's not talk about this right now, okay?"

I held back a sigh of frustration, but quietly agreed as I returned my focus to the game. I wanted more than *anything* to understand what was going on in his head right now. I couldn't focus on much else with the unknown questions about our future hanging around. I mean, my future was adaptable to his—I wanted to pursue coffee making. I was good at it, and the moment I got to try my hands at a coffee machine I fell in love with the idea. I could easily follow him wherever he needed to go, yet still do my own thing.

And I knew he wanted to go to Los Angeles to follow his music dream. There were many opportunities over there for him, but moving so far away would be expensive so he'd *need* that scholarship. I didn't know why he was holding back. He should have been *jumping* at the idea.

But I was going to respect his request for space. He obviously needed it. I just hoped he told me what was going on sooner rather than later.

After a half hour of solid gaming, I heard my Mom shuffling through the front door with bags of groceries. Ever the helpful one, Ryan jumped straight up to give her a hand, which left her beaming.

"Thank you, Ryan!" she said, as he took a handful from her. "Are you staying for dinner? We're having pork ribs with apple slaw."

"Sounds delicious, Caroline," he replied, with a big smile. Mom busied herself with unpacking everything and started prepping dinner, and although I could tell Ryan wanted to return cuddling on the couch, he stepped in to help her. So of course I went over to help too, not wanting to be left out.

The three of us were chatting happily together. Mom poured herself a glass of wine and showed Ryan how she got the apple flavour through the meat.

Ryan *hated* cooking, but he still nodded and did his best to do it the way she showed him. I'd told Mom countless times that Ryan hated cooking, and she'd always made it clear that he didn't have to help, but I think it was his way of helping out and showing that he wanted to be a part of the family.

A sudden idea came to me to cheer him up—a homemade espresso martini.

I mean, it was only fair if Mom was having wine that we had a drink too, right? She was pretty lenient on the alcohol as long as we were being safe. And it wasn't like either of us were going anywhere.

While Mom and Ryan finished up preparing dinner, I mixed and poured us both a glass, then took them over to him. He raised an eyebrow at me when I handed him his glass.

"Is this your way of keeping me up all night long?" he asked, his voice low as he smirked at me.

"What do you mean?" I asked, confused. He glanced over at my Mom, but she was occupied with chopping the last of the vegetables and wasn't listening. He stepped a little closer and brushed his lips ever so gently against the nape of my neck.

"If I'm too buzzed to sleep, I might be inclined to do other things with you," he whispered huskily, tracing a sensitive line along my collarbone beneath my Henley shirt.

My cheeks flushed red, but as soon as he'd said it, he stepped away, smirking at my reaction.

"That *wasn't* my intention at all," I spluttered, still flustered. In an attempt to recover, I straightened my shoulders and added, "But even if it was, you'd *still* fall asleep."

His jaw dropped as I gave him a triumphed, knowing grin and folded my arms. Eyes dancing with humour, he scoffed and mocked being stabbed in the heart.

"Ouch," he replied dramatically. "Well, if *that's* how it is, I'll just go home, then," he stuck his tongue out at me and headed haughtily for the door.

Still laughing, I grabbed his arm and pulled him back. His smile was wide as he let me puppeteer his body back to mine and looped his arms around my waist. I looked up at his face—his bright blue eyes, the way his black hair fell loosely over them, the angle of his cheekbones...and so many warm feelings flooded through my chest.

"You know I love you, right?" he said softly, eyes boring into mine. I leaned in and kissed him slowly, savouring the gentle feeling.

"You never let me forget," I replied.

At that moment, I heard a scuffle in the hallway and my dad entered the room. I hadn't even heard the front door open.

"Evening," he greeted, nodding at the two of us. He was used to catching us being lovey dovey when he walked into a room. Mom came up to greet him and his expression softened when he saw her. Ever since she'd been home again, it was definitely more evident how much he loved her, and he went to kiss her forehead.

Smiling, Mom turned to us.

"Okay, dinner's ready," she said. "Let's take it out to the dining room."

After dinner, Ryan and I, both a little more light-headed from the alcohol, headed up to my room to bring out the movies.

Once we were on the landing, away from my parents, he tugged on my arms and bought me flush against his chest, holding me close. His lips found mine and I could feel the urgency in his kiss.

He guided me into my bedroom and kicked the door shut behind him. As I backed towards the bed, he stumbled over my feet and removed his V-neck shirt, revealing his bare chest.

My heart was in my throat with intensity of the way he was looking at me—but then he smiled softly and my fears faded. I remembered the first time I'd done it with Ryan and I'd been so nervous, but he had a way of making me feel safe. A part of me still couldn't believe someone like Ryan had wanted me like that...but then it became *very* clear it was no joke, no fluke, but a reality I got to savour.

I especially loved the way he cupped my cheeks in his hands—there was something about it that felt like he was focused on *me*. Not just my body—but my entire being. He did it now, his hands softly grazing the sensitive parts behind my ears as he kissed me deeply. I felt his body press into mine and a soft moan escaped me.

In a matter of moments, he was kissing along my neck, my collarbone, his hands slipping under my shirt to feel my bare skin. He lay me down on the bed and felt my breathing increase pace as I focused on every sensation. He removed my shirt and our bare skin pressed together, our mouths meeting once more as we tangled together and freed ourselves of our clothes.

A short time later, he held me in his arms as we were drifting off to sleep, and I felt content. I couldn't imagine being anywhere else, or having anyone else in my life. I just wanted Ryan for the rest of my life.

CHAPTER TWO

AN UNEXPECTED GUEST

Aubany's POV

The alarm went off at 5 AM, and I groggily opened my eyes. The first thing I saw was Ryan's muscular chest.

Woken by the alarm, Ryan shifted and groaned, rubbing his eyes.

"Is it time already?" he mumbled, pulling me closer to him so he could reach over me and turn off the alarm. I was already going back to sleep, nuzzling into his warm chest.

Noticing this, he shook me a little.

"You really aren't a morning person, are you?" he tutted, but despite his words I heard humour in his voice.

I mumbled back something about him being crazy and rolled over. I felt him lean into my back.

"Come on, we have to get up," he said gently, kissing the spot beneath my ear. Goosebumps travelled up my arms and I groaned.

"I want to sleep," I whined, burying my flushed face in the pillow. He sighed.

"Aubs, I know you like to sleep, but we have to get up," he said, sounding amused. He pulled the covers off, exposing me to the chilly air and promptly climbed over me to get out of the bed.

I groaned in annoyance again and sat up to stretch. Throwing my hands into the air, I reached upwards until I heard a crack in my back. A sigh escaped my lips.

"I'm so tired, though," I muttered, slumping back onto the mattress in the opposite direction and pulling the covers back up.

"So am I," he admitted, and I felt a dip in the bed on my right side as he began putting on his clothes. "I'm going to use your bathroom real quick, alright?"

I muttered something back and felt sleep take over me again. A little while later I was being shaken awake again.

"Aubs," I heard. I smelt clean soap and the nutty scent of coffee. My eyes fluttered open and I rolled over to find a mug of coffee being held under my nose.

Like a kid on Christmas, I shot upwards in delight.

"You're amazing," I beamed, reaching for the delicious beverage. Ryan pulled it away before my hands could grasp the handle.

"This is mine!" Ryan protested, with an amused grin. "Get your own!"

I pouted, and he rolled his eyes and handed it back.

"You're lucky I love you," he said, as I plucked the mug from his grasp and shifted into a crouching position across from the bed, cradling it safely from his reach. He smirked at me.

"Melissa and Lewis are going to be here soon, so you should get ready."

I sipped on the coffee, nodding slightly but barely responding. He sighed, and stood with his hands on his hips.

"I wonder what you'd have been like if I wasn't here. Would you have even gotten up?"

"Probably not," I admitted. I finally shuffled off the bed and crossed the room to my drawers. I heard him whistle with approval at the sight of me only in

my bra and undies, and when I looked over my shoulder he was lounging on the bed, grinning as he
looked me up and down.

I couldn't help but smile. At one point, it would
have made me embarrassed, but now it sent a thrill
through me.

As I rummaged for a clean tank top, I finished the
coffee in a few long gulps and then proceeded to the
bathroom to shower and change.

Once I'd done that I felt a lot more awake, and the
sky outside was starting to get brighter. I returned to
my room and we grabbed our bags, then began lugging them downstairs to the front door.

My mom was up, a mug of coffee in hand as she
got ready for work. She passed us in the foyer and
smiled.

"Good morning, you two!" she said brightly.

"Morning, Mrs. Winters," Ryan replied with a grin. His gaze trailed down to his bags and suddenly, his expression fell. "Ah! I forgot something—I'll be right back!"

Ryan hurried off down the hallway to climb the stairs again, and Mom turned back to me with a serious look.

"While we're alone," she murmured, leaning a little closer. "I want you to be careful, Aubany. I know it's been a while since you last went on holiday, and I know what happened last time wasn't your fault—"

I cut her off, sudden chills going down my spine.

"Mom, I'll be fine," I promised hurriedly. "They haven't seen Courtney since she disappeared from the island. She's long gone. And those therapy sessions helped, too."

I paused, a feeling of dread developing in my stomach at mere *mention* of Courtney, and a flood of memories came back from my therapy sessions.

Quickly, I plastered a smile on my face to hide the discomfort. "There's nothing to worry about, so *please* don't stress."

The last thing I wanted was to make my Mom worry. Her green eyes were warm with love and concern. She ruffled my hair and said,

"You're right. I'm being silly. Go and have fun, honey."

I moved in and hugged her tightly. A thud from the stairs indicated that Ryan was back. I peered around Mom to look for him.

"What did you forget?" I asked, and noticed him lugging a huge case over his shoulder.

"My guitar," he replied, and as he came into view I could see the unique shape of it.

The two of us bid Mom goodbye and moved our luggage out onto the front porch.

When Melissa and Lewis pulled up in the drive-way in Lewis' Ute, we went over to greet them. Lewis was the first one out of the car. He had dark brown hair, and green eyes, and wore a brown, crew neck sweater. He flashed me a friendly grin. He was Melissa's boyfriend of a year and a half now.

"Hey there, Aubany. How are you?" he asked.

"I want to go back to bed," I said plainly. Ryan snorted from beside me, hearing the disdain in my voice. I could just hear him teasing me later about how I was about as adventurous as a sloth.

"I don't blame you," Lewis agreed, running an awkward hand through his hair. He glanced over his shoulder to the car as the door opened, and Melissa jumped out. She was *far* too energetic and vibrant for this hour of the morning.

"Where's your stuff? Let's load it up and get go-ing," she said brightly. I noticed even her hair looked perfectly curled and resisted the urge to shake my head at her.

Together, we crammed our bags into the back of the Ute with everything else they'd packed, and then jumped into the back seat. Melissa started the car and we backed out, heading on our way.

The sound of Ryan's voice stirred me from my sleep.

"So…how far away is this place again?"

An ache had formed in my shoulder from how I'd been leaning into him as I snoozed. I sat up straight and rolled the kink out of my neck, wincing.

"I told you, it's a four-hour drive. It takes about forty minutes to get up the mountain," Melissa replied shortly from the driver's seat.

I blinked and looked out the window to see leafy, green plants, tall pine trees, and a lot of native yellow flowers—all passing in a blur. My heart leapt a little.

The last time I'd been to a place like this was when I was so young I could barely even remember it. I could vaguely recall the scent of pine trees and the beautiful sunsets against the mountain ranges. This was much more my scene than some tropical island, that was for sure.

Not to mention that, from what I'd heard, the cabin itself was gorgeous. Lewis had spoken of antique rugs, wooden floors, a stone fireplace, and a library of books. Plus, it was a lot cooler for this time of year, but not so cold that it was freezing. It meant Melissa got to wear her skinny jeans, so she was happy, and Ryan got to wear his favourite hoodie—which I secretly loved on him.

Lewis put on some music to pass the time, and we all sang along badly to it. Well, everyone except

Ryan, because he was the only one who wasn't tone-deaf.

As we ascended the mountain, you could actually feel the temperature dropping and I leaned into Ryan for warmth. Before long, the trees were spacing out little by little, revealing the view of everything below us as we continued up the winding path. There was a carpet of treetops, and roads looked so small that they seemed like nothing.

When I was really young, I used to think mountains were always pointy at the top. Then my dad took me up to the mountains and my naïve, younger self discovered that they could host entire towns.

Blakesky was nestled at the top of this mountain, and we aimed to get our food from there. It was a ten-minute drive from the cabin, which was hidden in the woods.

We knew we had reached the town when we began to see houses and frequent street signs. I couldn't stop staring at everything. It was an adorable, quaint little town, with cottages and a camping ground and a tiny, corner store grocery. People were walking their dogs, playing on the sidewalk, and mowing their lawns.

We stopped for about ten minutes to load up with food from the grocery store. It was a tiny shop, not much bigger than my bedroom, with only bare essential items. Once we had food and supplies, we kept going—following a secluded road leading out of town that sloped down a little. We turned off into the woods on a dirt road, and continued onwards for half an hour.

Eventually, a clearing came into view, and with it the most beautiful log cabin. It had been built right on the edge of a slope, and you could see the mountains in the distance, on the other side of an expansive, glittering lake far, far below us. It looked like a painting—simply magical against the red hues of the wooden cabin structure.

Melissa pulled up on the gravel outside of the cabin, and all of us clambered out, eager to stretch our stiff legs and take a better look around. The air was icy on my skin and the scent of pine instantly overtook my senses.

"I bet this is beautiful in wintertime," Melissa said, her eyes wide as she gazed around. Lewis nodded at her, grinning, with his hands on his hips.

"It's magnificent. The lake freezes over, and the kids all head down there to skate."

"Let's go inside, shall we?" Ryan suggested. We all grabbed two handfuls of luggage from the car and Lewis unlocked the front door. It swung open and we shuffled into the quiet, inviting cabin. A musty smell greeted me, followed by the faint tinge of pine. A spacious lounge was just a step down from the main entry. Tall, wooden logs held up the structure. I looked up and noticed a mezzanine upstairs, guarded with wooden railings.

"Let's leave our things down here for now—I just need to clean out the upstairs bedrooms before we can get settled," Lewis said. "It's been ages since our family has stayed here, and there's likely a lot of dust."

He gestured to the lounge room.

"Make yourselves at home! There's a coffee machine in the kitchen and I packed some hot chocolate too," he said, before heading up the creaky staircase. I gave Ryan an excited smile, and he grinned back at me.

"Should we help Lewis?" I suggested, but Ryan scoffed.

"He's the one who wanted to come out here so early to clean—so let him do it. Let's go explore," he said, grabbing my hand. He had a twinkle in his eyes that made me grin—it reminded me of all the spontaneous things we'd done back on Nula Island seven months ago.

Somehow, I couldn't resist Ryan's infectious energy.

The two of us took off into a room on the right. It was a study, with big windows overlooking the scenery outside. A wall of shelves held rows of books—most of them based on historical topics, which made me wrinkle my nose. There was a finely carved desk with a comfy-looking chair, and two armchairs opposite that.

Ryan plucked a book off the shelf, blew off a thin layer of dust, then began flipping through the pages.

"Christ. Lewis' family has poor tastes in literature for what's meant to be a holiday cabin. Sorry to disappoint you, Aubs," he said, wrinkling his nose and throwing it my way.

My instincts kicked in and I caught it before it could plummet to its doom. Opening it, I discovered it was a textbook. The pages seemed aged as I turned them in my hands.

Ryan threw me a sly smile as I stuck it back on the shelf and added,

"Looks like you'll have to rely on me for entertainment instead."

He puffed out his chest. I rolled my eyes, then grabbed his arm to drag him to the next room.

As we stepped in, I spotted rows and rows of bookshelves and realised this was the *actual* library, like Lewis had said. Among the many books, there were board games and an abandoned chess board.

I strolled and brighter spines of books caught my eye.

"Ah...I found a shelf of classics," I mused, tracing my hand along the aged spines. "Perhaps I'll have all the entertainment I need after all, with the likes of Mr. Darcy."

I threw Ryan a wink as I pulled out a copy of *Pride and Prejudice*, and he snorted.

"For one," Ryan mused, striding over to me to pluck the book out of my hands. "Mr. Darcy has nothing on me. And for two," he leaned in to press a slow, chaste kiss to my lips that left me dizzy for air, "I know that you *hate* classics."

I couldn't help but smile that he knew that about me.

We found the kitchen after that, and Melissa was already unpacking the food she'd brought with us into the appropriate places. Feeling guilty, Ryan and I stopped running around like kids at a town fair and chipped in to help.

Lewis came thudding down the stairs soon after.

"All clear up there," he said. "I'll let you guys fight over the rooms. Except the last one, at the end of the corridor. That room is out of bounds."

"Why's that?" Melissa asked casually, rattling open a bag of cashews for us to munch on.

"It's got some structural damage in the floor-boards, and it's unsafe to go in there. We just never got around to fixing it," he replied.

"Oh, okay," Melissa said. "Well, I want the room with the best view!"

"That would be my room," Lewis replied, giving her a flirty look. "Because I *am* the view."

Ryan choked on a cashew, and I had to stifle a giggle at his reaction.

Just then, there was a loud knock on the front door. I frowned, but Ryan simply shrugged, and Melissa instantly averted her gaze, which seemed strange.

"Who is that?" I asked, looking in the direction of the front door, then back at them, but they simply shrugged.

"Maybe it's the mailman," Ryan replied nonchalantly. I stared at him in disbelief for a moment, before folding my arms.

"Ryan. Why on *Earth* would a mailman come here? This is a holiday cabin."

He shrugged and avoided my gaze, but I noticed the hint of a smile playing on his lips. That made me cock my head and narrow my eyes at him.

The four of us headed over to see who it was, the sound of our shoes echoing as we navigated past all of our bags that had been dumped in the entryway. I pulled the door open, but before I could get a glimpse, Ryan covered my eyes with his hands.

"Ryan? What are you doing?" I protested, reaching up to pull them off. Then, a familiar voice hit my ears.

"Guess who?"

I ripped Ryan's hands off and my jaw dropped.

Standing in the doorway were Savannah and Alex.

I screamed.

She laughed and tackled me into a hug.

"Aubany! I haven't seen you in forever!" she said happily.

"What are you *doing* here?" I asked, still recovering from the shock. She was grinning at me.

"Well," Savannah said. "A little birdy told me you were going to Lewis' cabin for spring break and invited us to join. It was a surprise," she said. I gave Ryan an inquisitive look, and he grinned back.

"Are you surprised?" he asked. All I could do was gawk at him for the first five seconds.

"You are the best!" I exclaimed, throwing my arms around him. "Do you realise that? I cannot believe this!"

"My grandma lives in Blakesky. It's no big deal. We arrived yesterday," Alex told me, running a hand through his curly locks.

I invited them in and introduced them to Melissa and Lewis, who seemed to already know they had been coming.

"Ryan called me to ask if it was okay," Melissa admitted. "I didn't mind, so I said it was."

"This is so awesome. You guys are the best," I replied, smiling happily. I hadn't seen Savannah or Alex for months, and I'd been missing them.

Savannah rubbed her arms and shivered. "Isn't it cold up here? I'm so used to being in warmer weather." She paused for a few seconds before nodding determinedly to herself and adding, "I'm going to fetch my sweater."

Melissa offered to show them upstairs so they could claim a room, and they began to hoist their luggage up the stairs. I headed over to Ryan and hugged him tightly.

"Thank you so much," I told him, and tiptoed up to kiss him on the lips.

"It's no problem," he replied, with a big smile. "I didn't want to spend two weeks having Melissa and Lewis as my only other company. I don't know Lewis very well, and Melissa still doesn't seem to like me very much."

He wasn't kidding. Lunchtimes were somewhat of a tricky situation at school. She never sent Ryan away, but she'd gone out of her way to glare at him for the first few months. Eventually, Ryan had made a point of ignoring it.

"She needs to get over that," I replied, folding my arms. Still, what could I do, really? That girl was so

stubborn that trying to change her mind was like trying to convert concrete to sandpaper. *Impossible.*

Once we'd all moved our luggage upstairs and
finished unpacking, we decided to have lunch. I had-
n't realised how starved I was. I hadn't eaten anything
since that morning, and it was mid-afternoon now.
Melissa and Lewis started preparing sandwiches in
the kitchen.

"It's pointless to cook something big now. We
won't be able to eat later," Melissa said. She handed
me a ham sandwich with cheese and lettuce. Everyone else got a matching sandwich, and we headed to
an adjacent room where there was a dining table.

"There's a raft under the house, too," Lewis said,
as we all sat around the dining table. "We should go
down to the lake later and paddle around on it. We
could even try and catch some fish for dinner."

Everyone decided this was a good plan. Ryan
was nudging me and giving me an amused look that

said *remember last time we tried to 'paddle' together.* I smirked back.

"With chips?" Savannah asked, looking hopeful.

"Uh," Melissa hesitated, looking over at Lewis. "Did we bring chips?"

"No," Lewis replied. "But you could borrow the truck and go get some from town. They'd go really nicely with fish."

"I love that idea," Savannah said. "Us girls can go do that while you boys catch us a nice, big fish for dinner! That way, I can get to know Aubany's friend a little better, too!"

"Sounds good," I said. So once we'd finished eating, we went our separate ways. The boys went out the back door to go get the raft, and us girls climbed into the Ute. It grumbled to life beneath us, and Melissa smoothly steered us down the driveway with Savannah in the passenger seat and me in the back.

"So, you guys met on the island?" Melissa asked us, as she turned out onto the main road.

"Actually, we met on the pier before we left—Aubany was about to vomit because of her fear of the sea," Savannah replied, smiling. I cringed at the memory. Melissa snorted.

"That sounds about right!"

"You know how I get around the ocean!" I snapped back, but couldn't help grinning.

"Aubany told me you were older. That means you're out of high school," Melissa added, sounding curious. Melissa was fascinated with other people's life stories and would always ask about them—even if you didn't want to discuss it. It was how we'd become friends. She saw my Mom dropping me off for school one morning and started bombarding me with questions about where in town I lived and what my parents did for a living.

Truthfully, it had been worse than a surprise pop quiz.

"That's right," Savannah said proudly. "I took a gap year and worked for a modelling agency. Just basic stuff; paperwork, a bit of coffee fetching, and they let me help out in the fashion department for a while."

"Was it worth it?" Melissa asked.

"It was...but it wasn't as good as what I'm doing now. See, I decided that I didn't want to go to college, so I stayed with them for another six months before my vacation. But when I got back, I got accepted into a bigger company—this time doing *actual* modelling—so that's what I'm doing now!"

"And she's *amazing* at it," I added, remembering back to all the photo shoots Savannah had sent me and shown me on Skype. Even her Instagram looked flawless and stunning.

"What about you, Melissa?" Savannah asked. "What are your plans?"

"*Well,*" she said, getting that familiar look of determination on her face. She *loved* being asked that question. "I'm going to study Law and Commerce," she replied, a little smugly.

"Oh, really! Why's that?" Savannah asked, looking interested.

"Because it fascinates me. I love hearing about those juicy criminal stories, and I love having my say about it. I want to make a positive difference in something I'm passionate about."

We'd finally reached the town by this point, and Melissa took a left.

"Alex's grandmother's house is just around the corner from the corner store," Savannah mentioned, peering out the window at all the houses. "But God, she freaked me out last night."

"How?" I asked.

"Oh, she has all these crazy stories about the town. Not pleasant ones, I mean. She must have told us at least a dozen of them--at *least.*"

"What kind of stories?" Melissa asked, sounding intrigued. A thoughtful expression crossed Savannah's face.

"Well, she was talking about this one family in particular. Apparently they had this huge reputation in town. The parents are dead now, and the kids are long gone. But when they were here, all this weird stuff would go down. Strange incidents—like local belongings going missing and kids being nasty to one another. When the father died, apparently the mother lost it and the kids got taken away into foster care. As soon as that happened, all the incidents stopped."

"That's kind of creepy," I said, shivering. Ever since Nula Island, I hadn't been able to handle much 'crazy' stuff. Courtney had left a pretty big impact on me, and though I was physically okay, mentally I still got nightmares and had breakdowns from time to time.

Being stabbed isn't a memory that simply *goes away,* and I had to be prescribed medication on top of seeing a therapist for the first few months. Ryan had been super supportive, and it had been a while since I'd had any problems, but I didn't want to go and purposely trigger any breakdowns or anxiety attacks again.

"I'd go into more detail about the incidents, but they were a bit too much for me," Savannah replied, still referring to the story. "Still, I'm kind of curious as to where exactly in town this woman lived."

"Well, we're not here to track down crazy families, Savannah. We're here to take a break from school," I reminded her, wanting to steer us *away* from crazy people.

"I know, I know..." she trailed off. Melissa looked interested too, but she didn't say anything. A strange tension filled the car, and I reluctantly wondered if I shouldn't have said anything. However, the thoughts soon left my mind when Savannah pointed to a building up ahead and added, "That's the store there."

The familiar grocery store we'd stopped at earlier came into view.

"Hey, Aubany," Melissa said suddenly. "Do you think the boys will *actually* be able to catch a fish?"

I grimaced. "Well..." I trailed off, and that was all the confirmation Melissa needed. She nodded determinedly and replied,

"That was my thought as well. Let's get a fish to be safe."

CHAPTER THREE

LOCO FOR MY COCOA

Aubany's POV

That night we spent hours talking as we munched on Melissa's lemon drizzled, grilled fish.

As it turned out, the boys *had* gotten down to the lake, but like we suspected, had come back empty-handed—so it was a good thing we'd thought ahead.

Once my belly was full, everyone began peeling off upstairs to bed. Ryan and I had already unpacked our luggage earlier in one of the rooms. It was gorgeous, with polished log walls, smooth flooring, and large beams that added personality to the space. The bedding had not only a hand-patched quilt, but a Sherpa blanket for extra warmth, and there was even a fireplace across from it.

I couldn't wait to spend time in there with Ryan.

As I went to wash up my dinner plate, he came to stand next to me.

"Hey, you," he said, carefully wrapping his arms around me and resting his forehead against my head as he murmured, "I was going to make a hot cocoa—do you want one?"

My eyes widened with delight.

"Yes, please," I said, smiling back adoringly. He leaned down and kissed me slowly and softly.

"Okay. Coming right up," he promised, his eyes twinkling, as he began shuffling around the kitchen in search of two mugs. I finished cleaning my plate, the scent of lemon still lingering from the detergent, and glanced through the arched doorway separating the kitchen from the lounge. Everyone had gone up-stairs now except us.

I turned back around and leaned against the island counter, watching Ryan busy himself at the stove.

"So, do you think there's a spa here?" I asked. Ryan glanced over his shoulder.

"A spa?" he snorted. "Aubs, we're in the mountains. Surely there are other things you want to explore other than a spa."

I grimaced.

"School's been stressful! And since my parents let me get a job finally, I've had money to spend. The last time I went to a spa was on Nula Island with Sav."

Ryan stepped away from the saucepan which was melting our cocoa to wrap his arms around me again.

"Am I not a good enough stress reliever?" he teased lightly, and I rolled my eyes.

"It's not *that,*" I replied, trying to ignore the way my cheeks heated up. "I was just curious. Why? What do *you* want to do?"

Ryan's eyes gleamed.

"I heard they had zip lining here!"

I let out a single laugh and folded my arms.

"You will *never* get me on a zip liner."

His eyebrows quirked upwards.

"Is that a challenge?" he breathed, and a rush of adoration went through me at the look of humour in his eyes.

"I hereby retire my 'thrill seeker' status," I teased back. "I want a simple life. No more surprises and life-threatening situations. Just you and me together. I could sit in a rocking chair on a porch with a book, and you could play your songs on the guitar."

"That sounds appalling," Ryan replied, wrinkling his nose as he leaned his hands on the counter behind him. "I would go crazy with boredom. You need a *little* adventure in there, Aubs."

It was my turn for my eyes to glimmer with humour as the corner of my mouth quirked up.

"I thought that was what the bedroom was for."

His eyes darkened a little, but at that moment the sound of bubbling became apparent from the saucepan. I jolted, peering around his frame.

"Ryan!"

Rushing past him, I grabbed a spoon from the counter to stir it. "You're not meant to let it boil like that!"

"Hey, I make hot cocoa all the time at home," he protested from behind me as I poured it into the two mugs. I shook my head and passed him a mug.

"I'd hate to see the bottom of your mom's saucepans," I tutted, and brought the beverage to my lips to sip carefully. It was slightly too hot, but it tasted fine.

"Shall we take this into the lounge and sit by the fire?" I suggested, and he nodded.

It was the first time we'd had the downstairs cabin area entirely to ourselves since we got here, and it felt strange. It really was a beautiful cabin, and I wondered what Lewis' family holidays here had been like in previous years.

"You know," Ryan said, placing his mug down on the coffee table before sitting next to me on the sofa. "I could just give you a massage if you're that desperate for a spa day."

I shook my head quickly.

"You don't have to do that," I said. "It was just an idea. It's too bad they don't have any hot springs here, though—*that* would be a treat."

"Any time I get to see you in a bikini is a treat," Ryan winked. I swatted him with the back of my hand and he laughed.

"I'm just teasing," he said, shifting closer to me. "Well, I'm *not,* but you mean more to me than just that. You know that, right?"

I reached up to brush his fringe out of his face.

"I know," I said, and my hand lingered on his cheek. Sometimes I wondered how I got so lucky to end up with someone like Ryan. I never imagined that guys like him could like girls like me, and yet here he was.

And he was *nothing* like the guy I'd built him up to be in my head before Nula Island. Seven months on from all of that, I'd never felt closer to anyone in my life. Ryan was the person I could talk to about everything, no matter what it was, and I knew he'd always listen.

"It feels weird being on holiday again," I admitted suddenly. I wrapped my hands around my mug as a shiver went through me. "I know this isn't like last time...but I keep remembering things from last time now that I have time to think about anything but school."

"And Mr. Hocker's terrible 'detention dance,'" Ryan reminded me, with a playful nudge, and I snorted at the unsightly memory—our gym teacher did this little butt wiggle when he caught students in trouble and it was *not* a good look for a man in his forties.

I was thankful for Ryan trying to make me feel better, but after a moment he sobered as well.

"I get what you mean, though," he said. "Everywhere I look, there's always that question in the back of my mind. *Is she watching us?* It took me months to get past it just being in my own house."

I nodded in agreement and remembered the conversation I'd had with my Mom earlier that day. Even *she'd* been worried.

After Nula Island, there was a brief portion of time where we had to talk to the police and give statements about what had happened. They wanted our help to try and find Courtney, though we hadn't been as useful as they hoped.

After that, they'd instated a temporary protection program for us, since we'd been her most recent target. But it had eased off quite a bit over the seven months, and now they just called us every now and then to let us know they still had no leads. Courtney was completely untraceable, to the point the police were even starting to circulate the idea that she might be dead.

But that was just another reason why I shouldn't have worried so much. It was like I'd told my Mom—Courtney was gone. It would be crazy to think that she'd come here after all this time. Wouldn't she have made a move by now if she had any intention of hurting us? She *had* to be long gone.

"Don't worry, Aubs," Ryan said softly, wrapping his arms around me. "I'll always be here to protect you. And you have Melissa and the others too. No harm is going to come to you here."

I nodded, smiling at him as I sipped my hot chocolate.

"You're right," I replied quietly. "I'm sure the feeling will pass soon."

He leaned forward to kiss my forehead, and I embraced the way it sent warm fuzzies through my body. With a single touch, Ryan could always put me at ease, and it was just another thing I loved about him.

CHAPTER FOUR

SCARY STORIES

Aubany's POV

The following afternoon, we were sitting around in the living room of the cabin when Lewis suggested going on one of the hiking trails in the area.

"We should do the big one!" Melissa insisted, clearly enamoured by the idea.

"But it's a whole hour and a half of walking!" I protested. I could already feel the burn in my legs and we hadn't even started. "And that's just to get up. Imagine having to come back down after that?"

"But imagine the views, Aubany!" Ryan teased with a smirk, but there was a hint of seriousness in his voice as he added, "They'll be so incredible. It's not much harder than the volcano hike we did."

The volcano hike had a proper path. This one would have more rocks and roots to trip on. And there would definitely be snakes.

"Come on, Aubany," Melissa begged. "I can take so many amazing pictures on my camera!"

I groaned and glanced over to Savannah and Lewis.

"What do you guys think?"

"We should give it a go!" Savannah said enthusiastically, jumping up from her chair. Alex nodded in agreement.

"It'll be fun, Aubany," he added.

Eventually, I gave in. I was just glad I had packed appropriate shoes. I know I sounded quite whiney about it, but I was hoping we could take some time to actually *relax* this week. I guess not.

We took Lewis and Savannah's cars and headed into town. The hike we wanted to do was situated near the local campsite, so it was easy to locate and didn't take long to drive to.

We parked in the carpark and grabbed our bags and water bottles. Ryan squeezed my hand reassuringly as I stood and waited for the others to lug their bags out of the car. Then we finally headed over to the start of the track and began the climb.

The first stretch wasn't too bad. We used the trees for support as we climbed our way up. The scent of damp earth beneath our feet was surprisingly refreshing and Savannah kept snapping pictures of us on her phone for Instagram. Still, I was huffing and sweating, and I knew we'd reached the harder bit when we got to the edge of a cliff and saw nothing but the lake miles beneath us.

The only way to continue was over a big, wooden bridge, which looked awfully rickety and had a long, *long* way down should it fall to pieces.

"Is this thing stable?" I asked Ryan worriedly, nudging one of the wooden planks.

He shrugged. "Only one way to find out," he replied daringly, grabbing my hand. Before I could protest or overthink it, he'd tugged me hard and was leading me across the bridge, with the others in hot pursuit.

My heart beat wildly as the bridge wobbled under our weight. I clutched the rope railing, feeling my legs turn to jelly.

"Ryan!" I squeaked, and he glanced over his shoulder and squeezed my hand again.

"Don't worry— you're fine. See?"

Despite my fear, he convinced me to pause halfway across, as if proving a point. The bridge swayed slightly, but didn't do much else. The sound of gushing water drew my attention, and I glanced out over the lake towards the cliffside to see a waterfall. It looked stunning with the late afternoon sun shining on it, sending rainbow ripples through the water.

"Woah," I breathed, and I heard Ryan chuckle beside me.

Then, the bridge shook again under the weight, making me shriek and shove Ryan so he'd hurry to the other side. I practically leapt to solid ground and collapsed, my legs giving out after the rush of exhilaration.

"Are you okay?" Ryan asked, coming to kneel beside me. My heart was still racing wildly.

"I'm fine," I breathed, reaching to clutch his arm. "I just haven't done anything so out of my comfort zone since the island."

He stroked my back soothingly as I pulled myself together, and we stood once more. This time, Ryan wrapped an arm around my shoulders as we fell in line behind the others and continued the hike.

Sometime later, we found a river we had to cross by literally walking through it, which no doubt led to the waterfall from earlier. I saw fish in the stream and tried not to step on any of them. They swam for their lives as soon as my feet hit the water.

"Hey, Aubany!" came a voice. I turned and was hit by a wave of ice-cold water. I gasped, my arms awkwardly rigid from the shock.

Ryan was cackling to himself from his splash attack. I smiled wickedly and kicked up a heap of water towards him. He dodged and splashed back at me again. I leapt out of the way—except I lost my balance on the slippery algae and fell on my butt in the cold water. Another gasp escaped my lips as I jumped to my feet, soaked and freezing.

Ryan cooed at me, still laughing. I glared at him as he strode towards me, but to my surprise, he unzipped his jacket and offered it to me with a small smile. I gratefully took it, wrapping it around my trembling figure.

"You guys, come on!" Savannah called from the track up ahead. She waited with her hands on her hips, and we hurried over to keep up with the others.

As we were walking, I suddenly noticed something strangely familiar. Up ahead, there was something visible through the trees. Ryan noticed it too.

A memory stirred in my mind.

"Look!"

I focused on the memory, trying to pull it into focus to make it clearer. The closer I got to the tree line, the more I was able to make out. It was...a cabin.

No, *the* cabin.

Lewis' cabin—visible from the hiking track. We'd literally walked so far that we were basically back home.

"Honey, that's someone's property!"

It came to me all at once— the memory of Renae, Ryan's Mom, scolding Ryan's dad, Josh, while we were on a hike. Both of our families had been there, and I'd completely forgotten because I'd been so young at the time.

I turned to Ryan, my eyes wide.

"We've been here before," I said to him. "I didn't even remember until now."

"I know," Ryan replied, nodding. "It was a long time ago, wasn't it?"

We'd been on a family camping trip over a week-end. My parents vowed to never do it again, because I'd spent the whole time complaining and bickering with Ryan.

The rest of the group didn't find it all so fascinating. They continued onwards, eager to get to the end, and we grudgingly followed pursuit, leaving the strange memory behind us.

When we finally reached the top, the sun was setting over the misty mountains, painting them in pastel pinks and blues. We found a small lookout, constructed of wood, and leaned on the railing to take it in. We were hot and sweaty, but the view seemed to make us all forget that. Even I was captivated by the scene.

"Isn't that beautiful?" Melissa mused, her eyes shining. She pulled out her expensive camera and snapped a few shots. Then she called Savannah over, and asked her to model for her against the background.

"Really?" Savannah asked.

"Sure. Maybe we could freelance it to a travel magazine?" Melissa winked. She snapped a few pictures, then made Alex join in for some couple shots.

Ryan came over behind me and wrapped his arms around me. He kissed the top of my head and leaned on it.

"Wasn't this worth it?" he asked me.

"It was, actually," I admitted. I always seemed to be admitting stuff to Ryan.

"Maybe we shouldn't go back down. We should just stay up here all night and look at the stars, and lie in each other's arms," he murmured in my ear.

I groaned to myself. "We can't do that. It's dangerous. And we can't leave the others," I replied, turning to face him.

He grimaced. "I know," he sighed, looking at me longingly. "Maybe we should plan a holiday just for the two of us next."

For a moment, I imagined what that might look like. Just him and I...where would we go that we hadn't already? Not another island—*anything* but that!

But then reality struck me and I shook my head.

"Maybe. But right now we have to focus on what we're already doing. Like college," I said, thinking about our future again. "Speaking of which, have you thought any more about that scholarship?"

"Aubany," Ryan groaned. "It's only been two *days* since you last asked me about that."

I bit my lip. "Sorry," I muttered. "I'm just worried. I don't want you to miss out."

Ryan held me by my arms firmly and looked into my eyes. "I can make my own decisions, and I promise I'll make a decision soon," he said. With that, he turned and headed back to the others, leaving me with a sense of guilt for pushing him again. I glanced at the others. Most of them were still gazing out at the view, completely content. But Lewis had wandered back to the path. He looked over at us and said,

"Come on, everyone. It's getting dark, and we need light to see where we're going."

"We just got here, though," Ryan protested, looking over his shoulder.

"We'll just have to come back," Savannah shrugged. My eyes widened.

"Uh, you guys can. But I'm not hiking all the way back up here again. Once I'm back at the bottom, I'm *staying* there," I said. Melissa shook her head, looking amused.

"Whatever floats your boat, Aubany. Come on, now," Melissa said playfully.

Ha. Floats my boat? Ironic.... I exchanged a glance with Ryan, who caught on to my thoughts instantly and was smirking. I was reminded again of why we were perfect for each other, and all other thoughts from the previous few moments were washed away.

~

Once we got back to the bottom and drove back to the cabin, it was dark, and we needed to get started on dinner. My stomach grumbled in agreement, and I couldn't help thinking how inconvenient it was that we'd hiked all the way up and down when the track was so close to the cabin. But even if we'd ditched the track, we would have had to go back for our cars.

Lewis and Melissa wanted to light the fireplace to battle the evening chill, and began to mess around with the matches, while Ryan went to find some food to cook—we were taking it in turns to cook each night. I couldn't help but wonder what Ryan was going to cook up, seeing as he hated it so much.

Savannah took a seat next to me on the couch and made a satisfied noise.

"Isn't this nice?" she sighed. "Just being here, doing something new. Seeing *you* again!"

"It is nice. In fact, it's been too long since we've done something like this," I replied. I heard bickering in the background and glanced over to see Melissa crossing the room towards Ryan.

"What's wrong with pasta?" he was saying, holding up a packet.

"There's no sauce! Besides, I bought chicken that we need to use up first!"

Ryan's expression became pained at the prospect of cooking chicken, and I considered going over to help him. But Alex suddenly blocked my view.

"While Ryan's cooking dinner, why don't we all get to know each other a little better?" he suggested, trying to lighten the mood as he settled in the seat opposite us. We all gathered around the fireplace. I felt a hand on my shoulder, and when I looked up Ryan was standing behind me. For a moment, I thought he'd come to plead for my cooking assistance. But instead he asked,

"Are you warm enough? Do you need a blanket?"

My eyes widened.

"I'm fine," I replied, smiling at his thoughtfulness. I rubbed his hand to let him know I appreciated it. "Are *you* going to be okay?" I asked pointedly, and the pained expression returned to his face. It took all my willpower not to laugh at him.

"I think I'll manage," he said, forcing a smile. He gave my shoulders a squeeze before proceeding back to the kitchen.

The sound of pans clattering and utensils banging in the background soon faded out as Alex began talking about the summers he'd spent visiting his grandmother here in Blakesky. Melissa bombarded him with questions about the best things to see and do, and then Lewis would back up Alex's claims, seeing as he had also vacationed here in his childhood.

But gradually, it all drifted off into other topics and before we knew it, Ryan was dishing up dinner for us all and there was a silence that had fallen over us. A comfortable silence, filled with murmurs of appreciation for the food, but otherwise silence all the same.

That was, until Alex piped up again,

"Does anyone here like spooky stories?"

Savannah jolted upright. "Oh *no,* Alex, please don't start. Your grandmother gave me nightmares a few days ago!"

"Well if you don't want to listen, you don't have to. But the rest of the group don't know about these stories."

"Is this the stuff about the crazy incidents that happened here?" Melissa asked, her eyes bright with curiosity. I felt a shiver go down my spine. With the cold night air settling in, the idea of incidents occurring in this very town was *not* something I wanted to think about. *Especially* if we were isolated in a cabin in the woods. I hugged myself in an attempt to reassure myself and my gaze drifted towards the wide cabin windows—which revealed nothing but pitch-black darkness outside.

"My sister used to be fascinated with those stories," Lewis pointed out. "She'd research them and talk about every new detail she discovered."

I raised an eyebrow.

"I didn't know you had a sister, Lewis," I said, frowning.

"Yeah, me neither," Ryan added, leaning forward with his plate of chicken and mashed potato.

Melissa jumped in, putting both arms on Lewis' shoulders as she added,

"He doesn't like to talk about her much. They don't get along anymore."

Lewis' eyes fell downward and his mouth pulled into a thin line.

"Well, the most famous story I heard was the one about a family that lived in this town," he said, completely brushing off Melissa's comment. "From what I know, there was a woman who lived here with a son and a daughter. The son was expected to look out for his sister because he was the older one. But the sister was always running off, doing her own thing, without telling anybody she was gone."

The way he was telling the story made it sound like an urban legend. Which meant it probably wasn't true, but it still gave me shivers. Everyone else listened with keen interest. Even Savannah, though she was clutching Alex's arm tightly. Alex was eyeing Lewis strangely—and I couldn't tell if he'd heard this one too. It was like an eerie hush had fallen over us all as Lewis continued on,

"No one could figure out how the strange behaviour started, but one day the sister became *obsessed* with finding a boy with black hair and blue eyes."

I could feel a sense of numbness coming over me as I listened. I couldn't bring myself to walk away or tune him out.

"Soon after, the brother began to help her search. Whenever someone who matched their description came along, they'd stalk them. Collect information on them. Anybody who got too close to them usually ended up getting mysteriously hurt. It was only when people began to disappear that the police got more involved. When they uncovered boxes and boxes of pictures, stolen possessions, and locks of hair, they separated the two kids. Apparently, the boy was sent to a foster home and went to counselling, but the sister...she had some kind of disorder. An obsessive disorder, but an *extreme* one. She was sent off to an asylum to undergo treatment."

I exchanged an uneasy look with Ryan, who had gone stiff beside me. I could see why; Ryan had black hair and blue eyes. And the girl sounded so *very* much like Courtney it was unnerving. I reached out to grab his hand and reassure him everything was okay.

"Lewis...what were their names?" I asked softly. He glanced over at me, then shifted his gaze to the ground.

"I don't know. My sister never told me that part. All I know is that the two kids haven't been heard of since...and the mother died a few years ago. I don't know whether the mother had anything to do with it—but it seemed strange that the kids were taken from her so abruptly like that."

There was an uncomfortable silence for a few moments, where we all did nothing but stare into the dying embers of the crackling fire. Lewis shifted in his chair, catching my attention, his eyes scanning all of us. They stopped and lingered on me, and I frowned at him.

"Did they find the missing people?" Ryan asked.

"I don't know," Lewis replied. "That's all my sister told me—I never thought to dig any deeper into the story."

Another few seconds passed before Savannah spoke,

"Well, now that you've all been informed on that, we should do something more uplifting. Ryan, did you bring your guitar?"

Ryan jumped up.

"Yes, I did, as a matter of fact," he replied, looking only too eager to get away. "I'll go grab it."

Ryan's absence at my side barely registered in my mind. All I could think about was how creepily familiar that girl had sounded. The one person I'd known to act that way was the one person who'd haunted my dreams for the past year.

But surely that *couldn't* have been Courtney? That would only be a coincidence. And even if it *was*...there had been tons and tons of victims, by the sounds of things. Meaning she's had a whole seven months to find a new victim; and though I'd *never* wish what she did to us upon anyone, chances of her coming after us again after *this* long were slim. The police couldn't find her anywhere. She was long gone, by the sounds of things.

When Ryan returned, he began to strum a song and everyone started to sing and hum along. All except me, because I excused myself and went upstairs to my room to grab my phone. I settled in the dark, on the soft mattress of the double bed, bringing a blanket over my knees for added warmth and, to be completely honest, a sense of security. I could hear Ryan's faint singing downstairs which was comforting in a way...though I wished he were here with me.

There wasn't much signal, and each webpage loaded slowly, but I wanted to do a check on Courtney's history. I searched for recent articles about her escape.

Seven months out of the asylum, and she still hadn't been found.

Seven months since she'd almost killed me. Killed *all* of us. Because of her strange obsession with Ryan.

Her disorder wasn't a common one, and details weren't allowed to be disclosed to the public for personal and privacy reasons, but every article described her disorder as 'obsessive' or 'uncontrollable' and sometimes even 'manipulative.' Warnings to stay clear of her and report her immediately popped up in every article too.

After some thorough digging, I found a bit about her history. A lot of it was, again, unable to be disclosed due to privacy issues, but her asylum was situated in the outskirts of Florida, a good five hours away from Blakesky and Tallahassee, in which I'd grown up.

Wouldn't she have been situated somewhere closer to home if that girl had really been Courtney? She was only young when she was taken away--or was she? Honestly, I didn't even know. All I was doing was freaking myself out. This was *exactly* what my counsellor had discouraged me from doing. In order to move on, I had to steer *clear* of anything concerning her. So I shut off my phone and took a few moments to clear my head.

There was a sudden thud from outside the room, which made me shriek. The door flew open and Savannah poked her head in.

"What's wrong?" she asked frantically.

I breathed a sigh of relief.

"You scared me," I replied, exhaling. My hands had balled into tense fists and I'd started shaking. Savannah noticed and her gaze softened apologetically.

"So I'm *not* the only one shaken up?" Savannah replied, flicking on the light switch. "Good. Maybe Alex will stop teasing me now!"

"I think that story hit me too close to home, with all the recent events," I said quietly.

"I know what you mean," Savannah nodded, taking a seat beside me.

We'd all been through the same thing together, which was why it annoyed me that Lewis had gone off telling us about those stories. Melissa and Lewis had *no* idea what it was like to go through what we did. Melissa was always talking about wanting to be in the courtroom. But trying to piece evidence together was completely different from witnessing or even experiencing it happening. She had no idea what it was like to go through the terror of something like that. Her enthusiasm and intrigue towards murder mysteries and incidents sort of annoyed me because of that.

And Lewis...I mean, he couldn't have understood it either, but he would have heard what we went through just like Melissa did. The *least* he could do was be thoughtful about what he said before saying it.

"I'm so freaked out, I just want to go to sleep," Savannah said, climbing under the blankets.

"Did you want to change first?" I asked, eyeing her dirty hiking gear.

"Oh," she said, looking down. "Yes, actually."

She got up and headed for the door

"Wait! You'll come back after, right?" I said urgently. "I don't want to be alone in here!"

"Yeah, I'll come back," she promised. Once she was gone, I decided to get changed and ready for bed, too, not planning on going downstairs again tonight.

I'd had my fair share of scary stories for one night.

CHAPTER FIVE

THE ADVENTURES OF BATHROOM TOAD

Aubany's POV

I'd been dreaming about lounging in the blissfully relaxing hot springs of a five-star rated spa when I was abruptly shaken awake—and felt as if I'd been drenched in an icy shower when the cold reality hit me.

"What the..." I trailed off, pulling the blankets tighter around me for warmth as a flash light flicked on and shone in my face. I heard a groan from my left, and startled when I realised it was Ryan shaking me from my right. As in, it was not *him* in the bed on the left with me.

A mop of blonde hair emerged from under the sheets.

"Why is the light on?" Savannah mumbled, sitting up.

"Why is Savannah in our bed?" Ryan mused, his eyebrows quirked up with curiosity as he watched her rub her eyes.

"Why the *hell* did you wake us both up?" I shot back at him, squinting and raising my hand to block out the light. "And get that thing out of my face!"

I reached over to the nightstand to flick on a light, but when I clicked the switch it didn't work.

"Power's out," Ryan explained, watching me struggle with the switch. "That's why I'm here, actually. We need to go get some firewood."

I looked at him as if he'd just asked me to run naked around the house.

"Do I look like I cut firewood?" I asked him dully. "Just come to bed. The power will be back in the morning."

"Yeah, no—Aubs, this isn't like Tallahassee," he told me, his hand on his hip as he grinned at me. "Without the power, there's no internal heating. We'll all freeze unless we get a fire going."

He gestured to our empty fireplace across the room with his torch. I stared at it, dread filling my gut at the thought of venturing outside right now.

In the dark.

And the cold.

"Have fun with that," Savannah mumbled, disappearing entirely under the blankets.

"You're coming too!" Ryan said, pulling the blankets off us both. I yelped as cold air hit me and hugged my legs to my chest. "We're *all* going. It'll be faster that way. Come on, Lewis knows a spot where there's already some chopped wood. We just need to go and grab it."

"Can't you?" I whined.

"It's *heavy*, Aubs. It won't take long," he said, and crossed the room to throw me a jacket. I caught it—it was a denim jacket. I wished I'd bought a snow jacket with how cold the night air was.

"I'll meet you both downstairs," he said, exiting the room. Savannah let out a huff, then climbed out of my bed. She must have fallen asleep next to me as we hid away from Alex and his scary stories earlier. I begrudgingly pulled on the jacket and followed her out onto the landing.

The entire house was pitch black, and it sent chills down my spine as I carefully felt my way along the wall to the staircase. I could barely see, and the house wasn't exactly familiar to me. Thankfully, I saw a flashlight beam on the first floor, so I knew I was heading the right way as I slowly made my way down the stairs.

"Ryan?" I called, as I headed for the front door.

"Here," I heard him reply, and found him waiting outside on the steps. My teeth chattered from the cold as I made my way to him.

"Let's make this quick," I grumbled, and followed him onto the gravel path. We crunched our way over to the forest.

"Lewis said it was this way," he pointed, guiding me further and further into the trees.

"Are you sure?" I whispered, looking around. "I don't see any lights, or any of the others. What if there are bears?"

Ryan snorted.

"Aubs, there are no bears out here."

"You don't know that!" I cried, my heart beating wildly. "If not bears, snakes. Or wolves. Or even a deer—"

"Aubany, *relax*," Ryan groaned, pulling me closer to hug me with one arm reassuringly. "You've faced worse than bears. You've tangled with jelly-fish."

"*You* tangled with the jellyfish!" I reminded him. "And you nearly died! I, for one, am trying to avoid death, thank you very much."

"Look, it must be over here," he interrupted, his flashlight landing on a stump with an axe sitting in the centre, and piles of wood surrounding it. "The others must have already grabbed theirs."

"Well let's grab it and *go* already!" I insisted, rushing forward to grab a handful of logs. I cringed as bits of bark flaked off onto my clothes—the clothes I intended to sleep in once I got back to our *gloriously warm bed.*

As I held the cluster of wood close, I felt something slimy touch my hand

I screamed and dropped the wood as I felt it travel onto my jacket sleeve.

"What is it?" Ryan cried, as I leapt away and shook my arms violently.

"I don't know I don't know I don't know!"

I flailed as Ryan grabbed me and the torchlight shone in my face. He let out a laugh and brushed whatever it was off my jacket, making me stumble away three steps.

"It's a wood frog," he chuckled, and his torchlight shone on a little brown frog as it hopped away into the crunchy overgrowth of the forest, blending into the brown leaves. I let out a long sigh of relief.

"I thought it was a snake, or a spider..." I trailed off, my heart still pounding. Ryan passed me the torch, and gathered the logs I'd dropped. After checking all of them, he handed off three to me and picked up a few more from the pile.

"This should be enough to last the night," he said, then gestured for us to head back to the cabin. He wasn't kidding—these things *were* heavy.

By the time we got back, and dumped the logs into the fireplace, I needed to pee.

"I'll be right back," I told Ryan, as he fiddled with a pack of matches, then headed down the hall to the bathroom. I was still shivering as the closed the door behind me, and I hoped that by the time I got back Ryan would have lit a fire and we could go to sleep.

I sat myself down on the toilet to do my business, and was nearly falling asleep in the dark when something touched my foot.

I screamed, leaping off the toilet and backing across the bathroom. I pulled my pants up and reached for the light switch.

Flick, flick.

Damn it, the stupid power was still out!

After a moment, I heard knocking at the door.

"Aubs? You okay?" came Ryan's muffled voice. I threw the door open and ran out past him—straight into Savannah's open arms. I nearly jumped out of my skin, not having expected her to be standing there.

"Something touched my foot!" I cried, bracing myself against Savannah's shoulders before turning back to Ryan. The flashlight went on again, and Ryan scanned the bathroom. Savannah peered through the door with him, then let out a laugh.

"It's a frog!" she exclaimed, her eyes landing on the creature hopping around. "How did it get in here?"

"*Another one?*" I shrieked in disbelief, as I watched it.

"That's a toad," Ryan corrected, crossing the room to inspect it with the light. It jumped away from him towards the bathroom counter. "The other one was a frog, Aubany."

"*Why are there frogs everywhere?*" I demanded. This *had* to be a joke! One of the boys was clearly pranking us. I bet the entire cabin was filled with frogs by now.

"Calm down Aubany, they must have been hiding in the firewood," Ryan said, bending down to try and grab the toad. It leapt away, hopping towards us.

A noise erupted in the back of my throat as I stumbled back. I felt so slimy and gross and I *really* wanted to shower now—but not if there were frogs lurking in the bathroom, of all places.

A mental image of a frog jumping onto my naked body made me shudder on the spot.

"Aren't toads poisonous?" Savannah asked, a quiver in her voice as she watched with wary eyes. It jumped near us and we both recoiled, our backs smacking into the balustrade. I held my breath, watching the toad make its unpredictable little hops and jumps in the narrow torchlight.

Ryan crept closer to it.

"Ryan, don't touch it!" I protested, with wide eyes.

"Well, I have to get it out of here—what if someone else needs to pee?" he protested, reaching for one of the towels and placing the torch on the bathroom countertop.

"Whose towel is that?" Savannah asked, as he crept towards the toad.

"Hopefully Lewis,'" Ryan muttered. He inched forward ever so slowly, holding the towel carefully.

Clunk!

The room went into total darkness, and Savannah and I both screamed as we clung to each other. The torch had rolled off the counter and hit the floor, causing the battery to fall out.

"*Where's the toad!*" I shrieked, dancing on the spot as I tried to scan the pitch-dark floor for it. A door creaked opened at the end of the hallway.

"What the *hell* is with all the screaming?" Melissa's voice echoed angrily.

"Argh!" Ryan cried from within the dark bathroom. "It's jumped on me!"

"It has Ryan!" Savannah wailed from beside me. *"He's being poisoned!"*

"What has Ryan?" Melissa insisted, and her own torch flicked on as she marched towards us. She shone the light into the bathroom to reveal Ryan hopping around on one leg, trying to gather the toad into the towel. It leapt off of him.

"What's going on?" came another voice, and this time when I looked the other way, I saw Alex standing on the landing as well.

"I think I just stepped on it..." Ryan moaned, looking around his legs for it.

"Ryan stepped on a toad!" Savannah continued to wail.

"A *turd?*" Alex frowned. "Like, on the floor?"

"*A toad!*" Melissa barked, throwing her hands up dramatically. She marched into the bathroom and snatched up a decorative wicker basket from next to the sink, emptying collection of soaps onto the floor. She lunged as the toad jumped away from Ryan and in one fell swoop bought the basket down over the toad, trapping it.

We all collectively heaved a sigh at once. Melissa rolled her eyes as she looked at us all.

"Thanks Melissa," I breathed.

"You guys are all *children*!" she scowled, stalking back to her room. "Go to bed already!"

Wow. I made a mental note to *never* wake Melissa up from her beauty sleep in the future.

Ryan gingerly nudged the toad into the corner of the bathroom with his foot, then grabbed his flashlight and shoved the battery back in. It flicked to life.

"I guess we'll take it outside in the morning when it's light," he shrugged.

I couldn't even wash my arms in the sink due to no power, so I followed Ryan back to our room. To my dismay, there was no fire crackling.

"Ryan, didn't you light a fire while I was peeing?" I asked, rubbing my arms for warmth.

"Oh, yeah...about that..." he trailed off, running a hand through his hair sheepishly. "Turns out the firewood is damp."

I stared at him blankly.

"So?" I asked, raising an eyebrow at him.

"So you can't burn wet wood—it's too dangerous."

I closed my eyes for a moment to process this information.

"So you're telling me," I said finally, folding my arms as I opened my eyes to glare at him, "that I ventured out into the cold in the middle of the night, was attacked by not one but *two* frogs...and it was all for nothing? We can't burn *any* wood?"

He gave me a sheepish smile, and gestured to the bed.

"I found some extra blankets, and we could always cuddle to stay warm?"

"Forget it,"

I stalked to the bed.

"Oh come on, I just tackled a *toad* for you!" he protested, following me.

"Yeah! And you're probably covered in poison now!" I replied, eyeing his hoodie and sweats.

"Maybe you'll get superpowers in your sleep?" he joked, and I deadpanned a stare back at him. His expression became serious.

"Look, I'm sorry—I didn't know the wood would be wet. And literally everyone else went out to get wood too, and now has to sleep without warmth."

"Doesn't make me feel better," I grumbled, climbing under the covers. They were cold from the lack of body heat.

He sighed.

"Alright, I'll go sleep on the couch then," he relented with a shrug, and turned for the door. My eyes widened as I watched his figure retreating.

"What? No wait—I wasn't..." I trailed off, and he paused. Slowly, he turned around, smiling slyly at me. I rolled my eyes and pulled the covers up further.

"I *do* want to cuddle," I grumbled, averting my eyes. "It's too cold without you here."

He simpered back to the bed, practically gloating now as he placed his hands on his hips.

"I knew you couldn't resist me," he taunted, and I regarded him with a dry look.

"Just get into bed, Ryan."

"In a moment," he said, and began pulling off his hoodie. He noted my horrified expression and let out a laugh.

"Wow, that's the first time I've seen that look on your face as I've been stripping," he replied. "Usually you're *delighted* to see these abs."

"It's *freezing*," I reminded him, my fingers clenching into the sheets.

"Well as you pointed out, I'm probably covered in poison from *Bathroom Toad*, so I'm ditching these," he replied, and dropped his hoodie to the floor beside the bed as he locked eyes with me, standing shirtless. I stared back, and his eyes darkened as I swallowed and let my gaze travel down.

"Like what you see?"

"I'd like it a lot more if it was in the bed," I replied pointedly, my eyes raking his body.

"You're quite demanding, you know," he teased, and dropped his sweatpants to the floor so he stood only in his underwear. Then he pulled up the covers, crawled under them and over my body, and cocooned us together as he nuzzled the crook of my neck.

"Feeling any warmer now?" he breathed in my ear. My face felt like a heater as I reached up to run my hands down his firm chest.

"You might need to turn the heat up a little," I murmured into his ear, and I felt him smirk against me. He kissed me firmly, and I leaned into his body, feeling all of him against me. I was addicted to every touch, every kiss, every moment I spent with him— even if he drove me a little crazy sometimes.

"Much better," I whispered against his lips, and he smiled as he kissed me again, and again, and again.

CHAPTER SIX

THE VOYAGE OF THE RAFTER

Ryan's POV

The sound of birds chirping woke me in the early morning. Sunlight was filtering through the windows.

Beside me, Aubany slept soundly. I didn't hear anything downstairs, so I doubted anyone else was up.

I lay there for a couple of minutes before it became clear that I wasn't going to be able to sleep anymore, so I opted to go for a jog and find a coffee shop.

Of course, I could make my own coffee downstairs, but then I wouldn't be able to go for a jog. And, to be honest, I could use some time alone—*especially* after all that Bathroom Toad chaos.

I threw on a shirt and track pants, then did up the laces on my joggers. Quietly, I crept down the hall, only stopping to scoop up Bathroom Toad from the bathroom, using a folded towel to keep him contained until I was able to get him downstairs and outside.

I blinked at the sudden brightness as I let Bathroom Toad out into the garden and placed the backet and towel neatly on the steps. My sleep-ridden limbs felt heavy and cramped, so I stretched a few times before setting off along the path.

We were certainly a fair way off from the town. We were pretty much hidden away in the trees. Not that I was complaining; I liked a bit of privacy.

The more I thought about that coffee, the more I craved it. As I inhaled the scent of pine trees and relished the early morning chill, I realised that Aubany would probably appreciate a barista-made coffee, too, so I decided to get two.

By the time I made it into town I was feeling much more awake. It was only a quick jog down the main street to the bakery before I was inhaling the smells of freshly baked bread and coffee grounds.

The lady at the counter took my order and went off to make a caramel latte and a vanilla latte. While I waited, I leaned against the glass counter and drummed my fingers on the surface. To the side lay a bunch of newspapers. A side article read:

Courtney Madsen Still Missing. Hentley Asylum Undergoing Security Upgrades.

I frowned with distaste and turned away. I'd heard enough about the incident at this point to last me a lifetime. Every time Aubany and I tried to move on, it was shoved in our faces again.

I quickly took the coffees and headed back to the cabin.

I wasn't game to jog holding hot contents in both my hands, and as a result it was half an hour before I returned. My coffee was already finished by that time, and Aubany had only just gotten out of bed by the looks of it. So far, she was the only one up, dragging a rug with her down the stairs.

"Hey, you," I said, greeting her at the foot of the staircase. She gave me a sleepy smile and ran a hand through her red hair.

"Hey."

"I bought you this," I handed her coffee to her. In my other hand I had the basket and towel, which I'd picked up on my way inside.

The coffee made her face light up and she leaned over to peck me on the cheek.

"You're so sweet," she replied, taking an eager sip. "It's the perfect temperature too."

"Really?" I asked, feeling relieved. I was worried it would be too cold for her by now.

She nodded and continued to drink it. We went to take a seat on the lounges, and I threw my empty cup into the fireplace, then looked around for the matches. Aubany was clearly shivering under her rug. The power was yet to come back on.

When I finally located them nestled with a stack of books, I lit a match and threw it into the logs. A fire crackled to life, and Aubany shuffled closer to it.

"So I never got to ask why you went to bed so early last night," I said, turning to her. "And why I found you in bed with Savannah—is she your secret lover or something?"

I waggled my eyebrows and she snorted.

"You wish," she joked. "No, Savannah was just feeling a bit freaked out, and I promised I'd stay with her. She must have fallen asleep."

"Ah," I said, nodding. I put an arm around her and she leaned into me.

"To be honest, I was sort of freaked out by what Lewis said too," Aubany said. "I know it's probably nothing, but the fact that all that stuff they were talking about happened *here....*"

"I wouldn't listen to anything Lewis says," I replied, turning up my nose in annoyance. "That guy doesn't have any consideration for others."

"I wonder what Melissa sees in him," Aubany muttered.

Honestly, I sometimes wondered the same thing. I hadn't known Lewis quite as long as Aubany. He started dating Melissa just over a year before I'd started dating Aubany, and back then Aubany had done everything she could to avoid me.

Despite having only known Lewis a short while, I didn't have a lot of nice things to say about him. Maybe I hadn't known him long enough, but he just had these habits that bothered me. Like, for instance, he'd constantly be looking at other girls. *Especially*

Aubany. Being a guy, I noticed it more than Aubany and Melissa seemed to.

But not only that. As soon as Aubany and I had started dating, the guy seemed to get jumpy around me. He didn't seem to enjoy my presence at all.

"You been working on any new songs lately?" Aubany asked me, pulling me out of my thoughts. I ducked my head a little.

"Kinda," I replied. The truth was, I *had* been. A *lot*. I had an entire book filled with songs, some unfinished, some complete with music notes. Most of them stemmed from my feelings about Aubany. I don't really know why I found it so embarrassing to admit this to her. I guess I just wanted to save those songs for the perfect moment. I knew that, if she caught wind of it, she'd ask me to play them for her. Or at least demand to see what I'd written about her.

Plus, most of them were uplifting, but a few of them lately...they were about my worries for the future. It wasn't something I'd come to terms with yet, and I couldn't bear to bring it up with her yet, either. She kept persisting about the scholarship, and I know her intentions were good but...well...I guess I was still deciding if there *would* be a scholarship. Or a future at all. Everything was so confusing at the moment, and I was so in love with her that I just wanted to focus on being happy. But I knew the longer I dragged it out, the worse it would get. Eventually, I'd have to make a choice.

"Kinda?" Aubany mused, already pressing for more details with a cheeky grin.

"They're not quite done," I replied. "I don't want to share them until they are."

"Alright," she relented, nodding.

At that moment, Melissa appeared on the landing above us.

"Morning, all," she chirped, perhaps a little too loudly. She stretched her arms upward and bounced over to us, looking especially vibrant today. You'd have thought the grumpy woman from last night was a different person entirely.

"I'm loving this weather. It's perfect to take the raft down to the lake!" she breezed.

"But it's freezing," Aubany replied, shivering.

"Wait until the sun comes up. You'll be jumping into that water in no time," Melissa winked. She glanced over at the fire. "Time for some hot cocoa."

"The power's not back on yet," I called out, getting up from the couch. I followed her halfway to the kitchen, but just as I'd spoken the cabin lights flickered to life around us. The switches had never been turned off.

Melissa raised her eyebrows at me from the kitchen doorway.

"Ask, and you shall receive," she mused, a glimmer in her eyes that made me roll mine. Talk about luck.

I'd learned that Melissa wasn't a big coffee person. She'd drink it, but she much preferred hot cocoa. Made in soy, apparently—as I watched her pull a carton of soy milk out of the fridge door.

"Well, if we *do* go down to the lake, we'll be fine as long as Aubany doesn't try any steering," I joked, referring to the kayaking incident which made us spin in circles. This made Aubany scowl at me from her spot on the couch.

"That was different," she insisted.

"Was it?" I asked, coming to stand behind her and smirking. She whacked me on the shoulder, and I playfully nudged her back.

It wasn't long until Lewis and Alex were up, and Lewis came down to tackle Melissa into a hug. A similar scene played out when Savannah finally emerged, rubbing sleep from her eyes.

We were one big, happy group.

Aubany went over to help cook breakfast, and while we were waiting we all sipped on hot beverages and snuggled with our significant other.

"You know, I've been thinking a lot lately about graduating, and college," Melissa said suddenly. "And I'm so glad to have met all of you."

"I agree," Savannah added. "I know we'll all stay friends."

There was nodding all around the group

"And it doesn't matter if we disconnect over the years. We've been through so many adventures together, and to have wound up here, at this moment in time...it's something special. A bond of some sorts," Melissa added, smiling at Savannah. The two of them had really warmed up to each other in a short amount of time. Maybe what Melissa was saying was right.

Maybe we were all bought together for a reason.

"Awww, you guys!" Aubany said. "Stop being so soppy! You're going to make me cry!"

Everyone laughed. I noticed Lewis and Alex grinning.

"To our friendship, and all the adventure that created it!" Alex beamed, holding up his mug of tea. We all clinked cups and drank deeply, the warm fuzzy feelings sinking deep into our hearts and guarding us from the bite in the air.

~

A few hours later, I had my board shorts on and a hoodie over a T-shirt. Aubany was still rugged up in a long-sleeved, but flimsy, shirt, through which I could make out her swimsuit. But I couldn't convince her to change out of jeans. She was going to regret that if she got wet.

Lewis and Alex lugged the raft, hoisted over their heads, as we made our way down the winding, overgrown path that led from the cabin to the lake.

"Look!" Melissa pointed, and we all peered through the trees. The sunlight made the lake shine and glimmer, and it honestly looked so refreshing and warm down there.

When we made it, the guys were only too glad to dump the heavy raft on a patch of dirt. Both of them were sweating.

"You girls can handle the rest, can't you?" Lewis winked, before taking off towards the lake. He eagerly ran into the water and dunked his head under. Alex wasn't far behind him, ripping off his shirt and following pursuit.

"You got this, ladies," I said with a sly smile, also heading for the water.

"Oh, it's on!" Savannah laughed. Melissa gave me a challenging look and added,

"You better start swimming, boys!"

She grabbed one of the paddles and made a threatening swing with it. Aubany was still hesitantly perched by the raft, eyeing a paddle with great discomfort in her eyes.

She was *so* having flashbacks.

I couldn't help but laugh.

The water was cool, and I took off after the others, who were heading deeper and deeper into the lake.

Looking over my shoulder, I saw the girls dragging the raft to the water's edge, and Aubany was inspecting for sharp rocks in their path. She was reluctantly attempting to shimmy out of her skinny jeans in the process.

Knowing it would take too long to blow up manually, we'd blown the raft up with a pump before bringing it down, so it was ready to go as soon as it hit the water's edge. Melissa scrambled into it and Savannah pulled Aubany in. Aubany tripped and dumped the paddles in the raft, a few slipping over the sides into the water.

"Oh, gosh!" she cried.

"Get them!" Savannah screeched from her perch at the head of the raft. She pinched one of the ones within reach and began to paddle. Melissa fished the rest out and passed one to Aubany.

The whole thing was so amusing to watch, but Aubany was quickly learning, and unlike last time, she didn't have any seasickness to distract her. A determined look on her face, she smiled smugly at me and that's when I realised I'd better start swimming. *Fast.*

"Oh, shit," Alex said from behind me, realising the same thing. "Your girlfriend levelled up."

The three of us started swimming as fast as we could.

The girls caught up to us fast, and they splashed us with their paddles. They relished in the fact that they were practically on a pedestal, up higher than us and wielding weapons of mass-splash-destruction.

"Get in here, you!" I growled playfully, tugging hard on Aubany's arm. She shrieked and leaned back, trying to balance.

"I'll save you, Aubany!" Savannah declared, wrapping her arms around Aubany protectively to hold her in the raft.

I splashed water up at them, and they ducked. While Aubany rubbed the water from her eyes, I grabbed both of her arms and she tumbled over the raft into the water.

"Gotcha!" I declared, and when she surfaced she let out an annoyed cry.

"It's *freezing!"* she shrieked.

"I know!" I smirked, before hoisting myself into the raft. The boys all followed my lead, and together we'd successfully taken it over, pushing the other two out into the water. They gasped at how cold the water was.

"Oh, it'll warm up," Alex insisted breezily. The three of us took off with the raft, paddling away. The three girls chased us, and after five minutes of pursuit we finally gave in and let them aboard.

Water rolled down Aubany's slender legs and arms as she took a seat beside me. Her hair was drenched, her top soaked; she hadn't been willing to sacrifice that much of her warmth on the shore.

When we'd all settled down, we set off to explore the other side of the lake. Melissa had brought food with her, and somehow in the rush to catch us she'd remembered to tuck it into the raft. Now, she was bringing out chips and two dips.

"Now don't go littering the lake," Melissa warned us all. "Or I'll kick you all up the butt."

"Yes, Miss *Greenpeace,*" Lewis replied, smirking.

Melissa frowned. "I'm serious! This place is beautiful and we have to look after it!"

"I know, I know, I'm just messing with you," Lewis said, chuckling and reaching out to bring her closer to him.

There was a huge stretch of flowers on the other side of the lake. Tons and tons of wildflowers waved in the wind absently.

"Oh, my gosh!" Savannah breathed. "I just had a great idea! Pull over on the bank."

We jumped out of the raft and dragged it ashore to ensure it didn't float off. Then we all followed Savannah as she led us through the field.

"There could be snakes," Aubany warned, looking cautiously at the grass. It was just like her to be cautious.

"We'll be careful," Savannah promised. "Everyone pick a flower that appeals to you."

Personally, I liked the forget-me-nots, so I picked a stem of these. Aubany went straight for a California poppy. Melissa found a Larkspur. Lewis picked a blanket flower, and Alex and Savannah both went for a cosmos.

"I'm going to make a scrapbook when we finish this trip," Savannah explained. "We'll dry these flowers and store them in the book, so they last forever."

"That's an awesome idea," Melissa replied, looking enthusiastic. "I'll print out all the photos I take and give them to you to use."

The two beamed at each other, and I glanced over at Aubany. She wore a huge smile with her friends, and wished I could make her this happy all the time.

But a nagging taunt in my head snuffed out the desire as quickly as it had appeared.

CHAPTER SEVEN

TORN

Ryan's POV

By the time we got back to the cabin, we were all worn out and all we wanted to do was relax. Lugging the raft back had been worse than getting it there in the first place.

We headed inside and put together some chicken salad sandwiches to munch on.

"So, this is adulting," Aubany mused, leaning over the kitchen counter and eyeing her sandwich. "Always having to cook for yourself. Always having to decide what to eat."

"What a scam," Lewis chimed in, with a laugh, and the rest of us joined in.

"You guys will get used to it," Savannah said, winking. Sometimes I forgot she was already out of high school.

After lunch, Savannah and Alex went off into their room for some alone time. I understood how they felt. Since we'd gotten here, I'd only had a moment completely alone with Aubany this morning, and even that had been short. I hadn't wanted to get into anything in case someone woke up.

Now, Melissa had gone off to snap pictures of some birds outside, and Aubany had gone off to change out of her semi-dry clothes into something a little more comfortable. I decided to take this opportunity to spend some quality time with her—and I knew exactly how I'd do so, too.

As soon as she was done, I grabbed my guitar from our room and asked her to follow me.

"Where are we going?" Aubany asked, eyeing my guitar. I smiled mysteriously at her.

"You'll see," I promised. Taking her hand in mine, I led her downstairs, outside, and through the trees until we found a quiet spot with a few logs to sit on. Wildflowers grew in a cluster nearby. It was a quiet, serene setting, and it was perfect.

I gestured for her to sit and unpacked my guitar from its case and my song book. I knew most of the songs by heart, but I still liked to keep it on me just in case.

She watched me with curiosity and delight.

Clearing my throat, my gaze caught hers, and she was looking at me in a way that made me feel so lucky to have her. I couldn't help but smile back.

"I wanted to sing you something," I said.

"I figured," she replied plainly, gesturing to the guitar and smirking at me.

I smiled back, then glanced down at my notes and felt a sense of hesitation come over me. But I'd come this far....

Taking a deep breath, I strummed the first chord and the music washed over me.

"Falling so deeply, into your complexity,

Stars and illusions that trap me here,

How did I find such a place that completes me?

And how can I live without you near?"

I spared a look up at her and she appeared fixated, listening intently.

"All I ever wanted is,

To kiss your alluring lips,

And now I get to do it every day,

You're a drug I can't live without,

The pulse in my veins,

And I want to feel this way forever,

So take every moment and,

Take all my pain away—"

I broke off mid-chord, suddenly starting to shake with nerves. This was the first time I'd ever sung an original song to her, and it was *about* her.

"Ryan," she whispered. Her eyes were shining with tears.

"Sorry—I shouldn't have stopped," I said quickly, but she had already jumped up and had closed the distance between us. I moved my guitar aside and cupped her cheek as she leaned in to kiss me. Within moments, she had climbed into my lap.

"I love you," she whispered against my lips.

"I love you too," I mumbled gently back, my kisses trailing down her neck. "You inspire me, you know?"

"Well, you bring out the best in me," she replied, her hands tracing up and down my back. "I honestly think you came into my life at a time I needed someone most. Because of you, I trust more. I have more confidence. I enjoy life. I just *love* you for so many reasons," she added.

"I never want to leave you," I murmured, pressing my forehead against hers.

But I might have to, my head reminded me. *It's the right thing to do.*

Resisting a shudder, I pushed those thoughts aside. I couldn't let them get in the way. Right now. That was all that mattered.

You're going to hurt her.

But I loved her. And I could figure something out, right? There had to be a way.

I knew in my heart that I got a thrill from singing. It was my passion and I'd had it long before I'd had Aubany. But Aubany...she changed my life. She meant the world to me.

I shouldn't have to choose between them.

Aubany gazed at me. Her beautiful, green eyes. Her fiery red hair. Her dazzling personality. How could I part with the fire in my life? My inspiration. How could I choose between her and my dream?

If you love her, you'll let her go, my head told me. *You can't let her put her life on hold for you. It's not fair. She deserves better. She deserves someone who is there for her every day. She deserves someone she can live with, not wait for.*

I knew deep down, in my heart, that it wasn't fair to plan a future with Aubany. Because all my life I'd wanted to sing, and I wanted to go away touring. And Aubany thought she could go with me to Los Angeles, and just be a barista. But it wasn't that simple. I'd be away *all* the time. For months at a time, on tours. And she'd be at home, alone--without me. If we had kids, she'd be raising them without me. If she had a bad day at work, there was no one to comfort her. I couldn't always call her. I couldn't expect her to change her schedule to keep in contact with me, or uproot her from her job constantly to come with me.

She believed she could survive on her own, but neither of us knew what it was going to be like out there in the real world. And in reality, our futures could drive us apart. The longer we continued on like we were going to be together forever, the harder it would be if we broke up. And in the end, I just wanted to protect her from getting hurt.

I couldn't be selfish. If I truly wanted to be a singer, I had to give her up.

But if I decided *not* to be a singer...we could be together. Which meant *not* applying for the scholarship. But was I willing to sacrifice my dream for her? Was she worth it?

Who am I kidding?

Of *course* she was. But sometimes, that wasn't enough. Sometimes, love wasn't enough. And I was torn because of it.

It seemed unfair. It had taken so long for me to get her—to earn her trust, and now...now I had to make the decision to let her go.

"Are you okay?" Aubany asked, looking at my expression. It must have fallen, and I quickly forced a smile.

"I'm fine," I said. "Just thinking."

She was biting her lip while studying my face. Her fingers traced my cheek softly.

"Do you think Lewis was talking about Courtney last night?" she asked suddenly. The change in topic made me sit up straighter.

"Why?" I asked slowly. Aubany's expression turned more serious.

"I just can't shake this feeling," she said, wrapping her arms around herself. "It sounded so much like her. And I know it's stupid to think she'd find us again. She's probably dead. But ever since last night, I've been freaked out, and I can't help but worry about it."

"Aubany, it's okay," I said, watching as she began to crumble in front of me. I held her tightly, shushing her to calm her down. "Even if it *was,* why would she come back here? And how would she find *us?* She's out of our lives now. There's nothing to be afraid of."

"Yeah," Aubany agreed softly. "You're right."

I packed up my things. "Come on. Let's head back," I suggested, offering her my hand. She took it, and with the other hand I hoisted my guitar case onto my back. I was going to have words with Lewis about this. Aubany didn't need this stuff resurfacing now that she was moving on. She had the future to look forward to.

CHAPTER EIGHT

ON THIN ICE

Aubany's POV

Later that day, just before the sun was setting, Lewis and Melissa came back from a walk to find us huddled around the fireplace chatting. As Lewis wiped his shoes on the doormat, Melissa crossed the room towards us.

"Hey, we just had an idea," she said, smiling. "Lewis was talking about the lake and what it's like during winter when the kids go down there to skate, and then he mentioned that there's an ice-skating rink in town. You guys wanna go?"

My eyes lit up. I hadn't been ice skating since I was a kid, and I'd *loved* it! I wasn't any good, but I'd very nearly gotten the hang of it last time and it had always plagued me that we ran out of time before I could perfect skating without holding the railing.

"Yes!" I shot out of my seat. "Let's do it! It'll be so much fun! Right, Ryan?"

I turned to look at Ryan, who had been sitting next to me on the couch. He'd suddenly gone very pale.

"Ryan? What's wrong?" I asked, dropping to my knees to grab his face and look at him. He shook his head.

"No. It's just...I uh..."

He coughed—the *fakest* cough I'd ever heard in my life—and said, "I don't feel very well. I think I'll pass this one."

A smile danced on my lips. *No way!*

"What do you mean? You were fine earlier," I pressed nonchalantly. "It'll be fun Ryan!"

He was practically shrinking back in his chair.

"It'll be more fun without me. I'll just slow you guys down," he protested.

"What's wrong, Ryan?" Melissa smirked, hands on her hips. "Scared of a little ice?"

He narrowed his gaze.

"Hardly," he replied shortly.

"Okay, time out for a moment," I said, and grabbed his arm to drag him up from the couch and towards the kitchen. I ignored the joking whistles that followed us and I steered him into the kitchen and folded my arms.

"What's the matter?" I asked him, my tone serious. "You're *always* down for activities."

I had a sneaking suspicion that I'd finally pinpointed a fear of his. But I have to say, I was *not* expecting it to be ice-skating.

He ran a hand through his black hair and swallowed hard.

"I don't like ice-skating," he admitted. "I went when I was young, and I nearly lost my fingers to a blade when I lost my balance."

I cringed.

"Okay, totally understandable," I nodded. "But this is a chance to overcome that memory and make a better one! You always pushed me on Nula Island to face my fears. Who would I be if I didn't do the same for you?"

"Yeah, this is really coming back to bite me in the ass," he muttered, and I laughed. Then I grabbed both of his hands in mine.

"Look, I promise I won't let anything bad happen to you. If you do fall, you just need to pull your hands into your lap as fast as you can, and then I can help you get back up."

"I don't know..." he trailed off, and it was so *weird* to see him look so uncertain of himself. He was usually so confident!

"Please Ryan," I begged, and he met my gaze with his blue eyes. "Do it for me. Even if you just go around the rink once with me, I'll be happy."

He let out a breath.

"I guess I could make it around just one time," he replied slowly, as if he were trying to convince himself. "Yeah. I mean, how hard could it be?"

I nodded enthusiastically, and grinned—and so it was settled.

~

"I've made a terrible mistake!" Ryan yelped, clinging to the wall of the indoor ice-skating rink. Loud music blasted from the speakers around us, and I snickered from a few paces down, also holding the railing for balance. Never in a million years did I think I'd get to witness Ryan so hilariously terrified.

"You can do it!" I cooed, holding out my hand for him. "One step at a time!"

His eyes were wild with terror, and his feet continued to slide back and forth on the ice as he held the wall.

"I'm going back!" he insisted finally, and my eyes widened. I reached out to grab his arm before he could make it off the ice, and he yelped.

"No, no, no, come on! It's not as hard as it looks!" I promised. He was shaking his head repeatedly now.

Melissa and Savannah came gliding around the curve of the ice rink and sailed past, singing along to the song currently playing at the top of their lungs. Ryan watched them sail by, and his expression fell.

"Give me your hands," I said, holding out my other hand for him to grab. He clutched the railing so hard his knuckles turned white, then took a deep breath.

"Don't let go of me," he warned, and I shook my head seriously.

"Why would I want to do that?" I teased gently. "I love holding hands with you."

His expression softened for a moment, then he shook his head.

"This is different," he said firmly, his eyes growing serious as he slowly grabbed my right hand, and then my left. He wobbled a little, and I saw panic flash in his eyes.

"Knees belt, stay calm," I said, and he slowly bent his knees. He began to slide inch by inch towards me on the ice.

"How do I stop myself?" he asked hurriedly, looking down at his feet.

"Um, I don't know—I'm not that good yet either."

His face paled again, and I could see the dread in his eyes.

"What have you gotten me into?" he muttered, as I let go of his right hand to shimmy carefully to his side. I grinned at him. This was *too* funny! I wish my past self from seven months ago could have seen this. She never would have taken Ryan seriously ever again!

"Ready?" I asked. His right hand shot back to the railing instinctively.

"Not really," he replied.

"And you say I'm not 'thrill seeker' material," I teased, as I tugged to move us forward at a slow pace.

"I never said that," he grumbled, moving his hand along the railing as we made our way down the first stretch of the rink.

Savannah and Melissa sailed by again, already on their fourth lap. I spotted Alex and Lewis on the other side of the rink, spinning round and round with their hands gripping a penguin—they were these little handheld figures that they gave out for beginner skaters to help them balance. Ryan was eyeing the penguin now with desperation in his eyes. Unfortunately, they'd snagged the last one available.

"You're doing really well," I complimented. "The trick is to sort of kick outwards—a bit like you're wiping your feet on a mat."

He watched my movements and tried to mimic them. After a few practice kicks, he realised he still had his balance, and I watched his expression shift to a calm focus. He did it a few more times, and I could see his confidence grow.

"Hey, I think I'm getting it!" he laughed, and I grinned.

Then he wobbled, nearly falling back, and gripped my hand so tight it almost broke as he cried out in alarm. I placed a hand on his shoulder to reassure him, but even my heart was beating. I wasn't that much better than him and he nearly sent me toppling to the ground.

Melissa zoomed past, cackling at him as she did a spin in front of him. Ryan simmered quietly, clutching the railing and glaring.

"I'm never going to make it around the rink," he said, and I scowled.

"Yes, you are," I insisted. "Look, you're still upright. You can do this. Let's take it slow and keep going."

He hesitated, then looked back the way he'd come and saw how much progress we'd already made. He turned back to me and nodded, so we began again. I basically dragged him for the rest of the first stretch as he glided along the ice, only moving to correct his stance when his legs began to split apart.

Then we reached the corner, and the ice wasn't as smooth on the corners. Unless he wanted to go over the bumps, he'd have to let go of the wall.

"You can do it," I said. "On three...ready? One, two, three!"

He pushed off from the wall and yelled as we sailed across the short stretch of ice. As soon as he could grab the handrail again, he did, then let out an exhilarated laugh.

"I can't believe I made it this far," he admitted, with a bewildered laugh.

"You're doing amazing!" Savannah called out as she skated past, giving him a thumbs up. She glided over to bop Alex on the head, who was still spinning in circles with Lewis.

"Better than those two, even," I noted, watching them spin closer and closer to the centre of the rink. I wondered if they were doing it on purpose of if they actually couldn't stop. It looked like they were on a roundabout at the playground.

We continued on through the second, shorter stretch of the ring, and then halfway through the third before Ryan had his second loss of balance. This time, he was calmer about it, and he still didn't fall.

"Keep going like this and you'll be a pro. Maybe you could even do figure skating," I told him.

He snorted.

"No chance," he replied, smirking at me. The song changed overhead, and colourful lights came over the rink to light it up.

"But, if I could skate properly, I'd at least dance with you here," Ryan added. We were far from doing anything like that though—the two of us hogged the railing and skated so slowly that everyone had to overtake us.

"There will be plenty of other times to dance," I smiled back. "Like prom! And homecoming."

"Oh yeah!" he mused. "I almost forgot that those were coming up."

I certainly hadn't. I was already thinking about what dress I'd wear to each one.

"Hey, what song is this?" I asked, listening to the lyrics. It was an electronic song, a little slower than the others, and while the beat was still vibrant the lyrics were gloomier.

"I've never heard it," Ryan replied, and we listened together. The lyrics talked about how sometimes love wasn't enough, and the singer was pondering on where dreams went to die.

"Did my love go to die on the train? Did it go to die in the rain?"

"This is kind of depressing," I commented, as the singer debated if his love had gone and died in his kitchen or his bathroom. "I hope your songs aren't as depressing as this."

Ryan snickered.

"Some of them are—sorry to disappoint you."

We made it to the fourth stretch, and Ryan's gaze was locked onto the exit gate. We inched closer, and closer, and then finally we reached it.

"You did it!" I exclaimed to Ryan, and he hugged me.

"I couldn't have done it without you. I mean it," he said, and I laughed.

When he ceased hugging me, I caught him looking at the rink longingly, and I cocked my head.

"Did you...maybe want to go around again?" I asked, raising an eyebrow at him. He seemed to consider it.

Then I heard a *bang*, and looked over my shoulder to see Lewis and Alex had spun into the wall of the ice rink and were both sitting on their butts.

Ryan immediately shook his head at the sight.

"Nope. I'm good," he said quickly, and hobbled off the ice. I laughed as he went over to sit and remove his skates, and I felt a hand tap on my shoulder. Spinning around, I saw Savannah and Melissa standing behind me.

"Come skate with us!" Savannah beamed.

"Yeah, now that you don't have Ryan holding you back," Melissa winked.

"I'm not that good," I warned them, but they just laughed and went to grab my hands at either side.

"We got you," Melissa promised, and the three of us took off around the rink together to the beat of a Taylor Swift song.

CHAPTER NINE

HARD DECISIONS

Ryan's POV

Later that night, we were stargazing, our rugs all laid out on the grass out the back, where a lit fire pit was situated. We watched sparks float up in the air and crackle into nothing. I tried to make out shapes in the stars, and looked over at Aubany to point out a constellation that looked like a starfish.

She was shivering, and I realised it *was* kind of cold.

"I can't focus," she said apologetically, sitting up. "I'm going to go to bed. It's warmer there."

After bidding me goodnight, she headed back into the cabin. I watched her go, feeling a long sense of admiration for her after how she'd helped me today.

I had never intended to go ice skating again my life, and the fact that she helped me get around the rink without falling once had done wonders for my self-esteem.

She really was amazing.

Melissa and Lewis were snuggling, but Savannah was toasting a marshmallow. Looking between Melissa and Savannah, I tried to decide who would be best to talk to.

Melissa had been friends with Aubany since they were kids, so her opinion was more valid than Savannah's. But I also knew she disliked me, so her opinion would likely be biased.

Savannah, on the other hand, seemed like an advice giving type of person, and I was drawn to that, so I ended up going over to her.

"Hey," I greeted. "Mind if I talk to you?"

"Sure," she replied cheerily. "What's up?"

"It's about Aubany," I confessed. Savannah listened intently to my problem.

"I love her so much, and she's completely changed my life...but despite my love for her....."

I hesitated, finding it more difficult to say aloud than I thought it would be. It was even harder after all the fun we'd had together today.

"I want to follow my dream and become a singer. I *need* to do it. I've been holding back, keeping this from her. I haven't made a decision yet about how to move forward because I'm afraid I'll only hold her back if I pursue my dream *and* date her."

"What do you mean?" Savannah asked, looking confused.

"Well, I'll be going away on tours, and she's got it in her head that she can adapt her lifestyle to mine. But you know what she's like. She'll sacrifice whatever she needs to in order to make us work. She'll sacrifice *everything* if it means coming with me. If she can't handle being on her own when I'm away, she'll come with me. Which means she can't be a barista, and I don't want to put her life on hold while I live mine. I want to be with her...but I can't hold her back."

Savannah thought this through. "You know...I think you have a point," she replied. "Aubany *is* like that. On Nula Island she risked her *life* to save you. She would be the kind of person to give up everything to be with you. As much as I admire that, I don't think it's right for her to do that. But she will. Because that's who she is."

My heart sank as she confirmed exactly what I knew all along.

"Exactly. And I can't live with myself knowing that," I said softly. "I don't want to hurt her. I want us to work out. But if I drag this on, it will only be harder later. If I end it now, I'll never know if we could have made it work."

"Ryan, I'm so sorry," Savannah said. "But I can't make this decision for you."

I grimaced. I knew that. I just needed some guidance.

"All I can suggest is that you make a decision by the end of this week. You have to apply for that scholarship soon, so why not set the deadline for when you get back? If you don't think you can part with her, you might have to find a way to compromise to be with her."

"How would I do that?" I asked.

"Well, you could limit your years singing. After, say, six years, promise her a lifetime. You can still release the occasional song or album, but limit your tours. Or maybe give up tours altogether. You'll have to make sacrifices here and there. And if you can't...then you have to give her up."

Savannah was right, but it wasn't that easy. I wasn't the one who got to call the shots. There were contracts involved--it just got more and more complicated. As much as the reality hurt, I had to do this. It hurt to think that after seven amazing months, I would never have more memories with her like the ones I have. The idea of breaking her heart broke my own. But I knew that it was for the best.

I had a week to decide. At the end of the week, everything was going to change—one way or the other.

CHAPTER TEN

TAMPERING WITH FATE

Aubany's POV

I shivered from the cold. It was hard to sleep with this icy chill in the air. It was warmer than last night at least, but not by much.

Pulling the sheets tighter around me, I tried desperately to fall asleep. The sooner the morning came, the sooner I'd be warm again.

There was a noise from outside, and I figured it was Savannah or Melissa coming upstairs. Then the door opened, and there were dull footsteps.

"Aubs?" came a voice. My eyes opened.

"Ryan?" I asked. Ryan shut the door and made his way over to the bed. Crawling in with me, he wrapped his arms around me. I immediately sank into his warmth. He smelt like pine and bonfire smoke from being outside.

"Oh, God, you're like a heater," I mumbled, grateful for the warmth. He buried his head into my neck.

"Your skin is freezing," he said softly. He started kissing up my neck, and I could tell he was trying to warm me up faster. Heat flushed to my cheeks.

"There's something I want to tell you," he said suddenly, placing his hands on either side of me so that he was looking down at me.

"And what's that?" I asked, tracing lines from his wrist to his elbow.

"I love you," he said earnestly. "And I will *always* love you. No matter what happens."

There was something in his voice that made me frown. Something I'd never heard before, like a pang of sadness.

I sat up and focused on his face, which was hard in the dark.

"What's going on?" I asked slowly. Ryan frowned.

"Nothing," he insisted gently. "I just wanted to make sure you knew."

His thumb rubbed slow circles in the palm of my hand. I'd had many, *many* conversations with Ryan about our love for each other, and he *knew* I knew. But this time was different, and I could tell something was really wrong. It unnerved me.

But he seemed intent on keeping whatever it was a secret from me. Just like he seemed so intent on not discussing our future, and not talking to me about his decisions with the scholarship. Maybe he felt guilty about that. Maybe he was trying to make up for it, or reassure me. But the fact that he *wasn't* confiding in me about his worries...it made me sad. I felt like he didn't trust me enough, or he didn't feel like I'd care. We were in this together—I wanted to be there for him in *everything*.

His expression was soft and loving. He leaned in to kiss me, his kiss slow and sensual. He continued to kiss me, his hands tracing my cheeks and travelling down to my arms like he couldn't get enough of me. Like he was trying to savour every moment we had together.

It didn't take long for me to forget all my worries and melt into the moment as he lay me down against the pillows. I tried not to let this happen too often— I didn't want Ryan's solution for every issue we had as a couple to be sex. But I'd already tried talking to him and, to be honest, he was just a little too sexy to resist.

Especially when his hand slipped beneath my pyjama pants and under my waistband to touch me *there*.

He watched me intently as my eyes fluttered closed and my lips parted slightly. I arched into him as his fingers worked slowly, the feeling building gradually as he increased his pace. His teeth grazed my ear, eliciting a gasp from me, and my nails dug into his shoulders. He groaned softly in my ear.

"Aubany," he growled, and at this point I was breathing heavily, the coil of pleasure from his touch driving me closer and closer to the edge.

Everything else was forgotten as my mind went hazy with desire.

"Ryan," I whimpered, bringing him flush against me and kissing him hard. He immediately understood that I needed more, and began removing the rest of his clothes. I shimmied out of my own, and then his warm body was on mine. I loved everything about it—the soft curve of his waist, the feel of his firm shoulder blades when I gripped them, the way he seemed to fit *perfectly* with my body. My arms could wrap around him comfortably, and when we were moving together....

The first thrust always made me gasp, and every movement after was bliss. I buried my head in the crook of his neck, lost in every sweet sensation. I loved the way he let himself get lost in it, the way he would grunt towards the end as my head tipped back against the pillows.

And then, when it was over, he would always hold me for a few minutes as we caught our breath. I held him tight and close to me, nuzzling against his sweaty skin and pressing kisses against his neck and chest.

He slid off of me and pulled me into his embrace so that we were lying side by side, reaching for the covers to ensure we didn't freeze later. Then, he stroked my hair until I fell asleep in his arms.

~

When I awoke I could hear voices downstairs. It was bright—morning had come, and to my left Ryan was still asleep.

I gathered some clothes and toiletries and, after slipping a robe on, headed down the hallway to the bathroom with the intention of taking a shower. Peering over the railing, I noticed that Savannah and Alex were the only ones up, and both of them were huddled around the fireplace. Alex was reading aloud from a book while Savannah painted her nails.

The bathroom down the hall was locked and occupied. I groaned in annoyance. I didn't really want to wait—especially after last night—and I was ready to go. So I continued down the hall and found myself facing the out-of-bounds room at the very end. It was pretty far off from the other rooms, to be completely honest. To the right of it was another door—not a bedroom. I opened it, and discovered another, smaller bathroom. Relief washed over me, and I slipped inside.

This bathroom was strange—the shower was in a separate room down the end, for some reason. I drew closer to it, and suddenly realised I could hear water running. My cheeks went red with embarrassment—*someone was already in here!*

I wanted to run for the door, but all of a sudden the water shut off and I freaked out. I spotted a nearby built-in cupboard and dashed in there, not wanting to seem like a pervert. I huddled among shelves filled with towels and soaps and clicked the door shut.

I had *no* clue if it was Melissa or Lewis in here, but I could only imagine the embarrassment if Lewis walked out naked.

I heard the sound of shuffling as the door to the shower room creaked open. It was pitch black except for a tiny sliver of light, so it was impossible to see who it was. *Not* that I was looking or anything. Still, my cheeks went red with embarrassment at the very thought of what I might see.

I heard a low voice. A muttering sound. Like whoever was in the bathroom was *talking* to themselves. Frowning, I pressed my ear to the door, trying to make out the sound. But the cupboard muffled the words, and when the sink's tap turned on, that made it even harder. Still, by straining hard, I managed to make out a few words.

"...It's too hard," the voice said. "...need to separate...can't get hold..."

What on *earth* was this person on about? Were they having trouble opening a shampoo bottle or something? I almost laughed to myself. *Been there.*

It sounded like a girl's voice. It must have been Melissa. She probably wouldn't have minded as much if I'd walked in on her, but, boy, would it look strange if I popped out of the closet now! I had to stay where I was.

"...are you still there?"

I froze. Was she talking to *me?*

There was a gasp and something fell to the floor. I heard it clatter and slide over to where the cupboard was. I peered through the crack and made out a phone. It had shattered on impact with the floor, and I heard a loud curse.

I widened my eyes. I could see the caller ID on the screen, though it was cracked and hard to make out. Bending down carefully in the cupboard, I made out the name.

Lewis Kellington.

I frowned. Had Melissa been trying to dirty talk him in the shower or something? And wasn't the other bathroom occupied? Maybe they were *both* sexting in the shower.....

Oh, that was so *gross*. I mean, I don't even want to *know* what they were trying to *separate*.

But still...why not just take a shower together?

Whatever, I thought to myself. I wasn't about to squat here questioning Lewis and Melissa's sex life. If they wanted to sext from different showers, then good for them, I guess.

I saw a hand snatch up the phone and I heard footsteps getting fainter and fainter. The sound of a shutting door sounded, and I breathed a sigh of relief. I stepped out of the cupboard and checked the coast was clear.

I'd only just set my toiletries down and was preparing to strip when someone else barged in. I looked over and saw Melissa, still in her sleepwear, hair dry, and looking shocked to see me.

"Oh! Sorry, I was just coming to take a shower. The other bathroom is in use," she said. I frowned.

"Weren't you just in here?" I asked. She frowned.

"Um, no. I literally just got out of bed."

A cold feeling washed over me. If that was the case...who had that been on the phone with Lewis—who I assumed was in the other shower?

I frowned, ideas going through my head.

Savannah and Alex were downstairs.

Ryan was still asleep.

So who had been in here?

"Aren't you and Lewis sharing a room?" I asked, narrowing my eyes.

"Well, yeah, but he's in the other shower—I think. Unless he's out getting firewood and it's Ryan in the other shower," Melissa replied, tapping a finger to her chin as she contemplated.

No way. No *freaking* way! I was in shock. I couldn't believe what I was hearing. The only plausible explanation was that someone *else* was in the house with us, and that person knew Lewis.

Was it possible that Lewis was *cheating* on Melissa? Did he hook up with someone in the middle of the night, and it just so happened that they hadn't left yet?

The *nerve* of him! Doing that right under our noses! Anger bubbled in my veins at the mere thought of it.

If he *was* cheating, I was going to find out about it and bust his ass. *Nobody* cheated on my best friend!

"Well, anyway, let me know when you're finished," Melissa said, completely oblivious to my realization. She shut the door behind her on her way out. I was still standing there, fingernails digging into my clenched palm.

I couldn't tell her—not yet. I needed some solid evidence or she'd think I was making crazy accusations.

I still felt gross and it was distracting, so I took the quickest shower of my life so as not to hold Melissa up, and then stormed out of the bathroom. Out of seven bedrooms, including the out-of-bounds one, three were in use. I thoroughly checked the other three, and found that they were all empty. Which left me with only one remaining option.

My eyes landed on the out-of-bounds bedroom, and I found myself having second thoughts on whether to go in there or not. I would be betraying Lewis--but then again, what if he really *had* betrayed Melissa? What if this was the only way to find out?

Or, perhaps I was just going crazy. After all, I'd been paranoid over these past few days.

I shook away my doubts. *No.* I had to check this room.

I reached out and grasped the handle, but it wouldn't budge. It was locked. If that wasn't suspicious, I didn't know *what* was.

I glanced around nervously. There was no one around, but if anyone saw me trying to get into that room, there'd surely be questions asked. And I couldn't go asking for a key.

I would have to find another way in. Perhaps from an outside window?

I briskly walked across the landing towards the staircase, but to my great disappointment, I spotted Lewis coming in the front door at that moment. I couldn't go snooping with him around.

His hair was wet like he'd just showered, and he carried an armful of firewood, which he dumped in the flickering fireplace to rekindle it. The others thanked him as he settled into a chair to chat with them.

He seemed so natural. It made my blood simmer again because I *knew* he was hiding something. But not for long.

I was going to get to the bottom of this.

~

"What are we up to today?" I asked the others, getting up to make myself a coffee. We'd just finished eating a breakfast of avocado toast, served up by a cheerful Savannah.

Melissa shrugged. "I haven't thought of anything yet," she replied. She looked over to Lewis, ever so trusting. "What do you think we should do?"

Lewis' expression turned thoughtful. "Well...they have rental bikes in town. Maybe we could ride on the track?"

Melissa clasped her hands together, looking excited. "This sounds like fun," she said excitedly. "We could take so many pictures for Savannah's scrap-book!"

Melissa got to her feet and began to collect all the dishes from everyone.

"I'll finish up here. Let's be ready to leave in about five minutes, okay?"

We all got to our feet and went to fetch our bags. Savannah and Alex, who were still in their pyjamas, went upstairs to change.

Once everyone was ready, we all headed into town. Melissa drove again, following Lewis' directions to the bike rental place. Narrowing my eyes at him, I resisted the urge to say something. I considered sharing my discovery with Savannah or Ryan, but decided that if anyone was going to hear about it, Melissa should first, so I kept it to myself.

"Hurry up, Aubs!" Ryan sang, as he sped along the track ahead of me. Lewis had not been kidding when he said the path had fantastic views—the track was created on the very outline of Blakesky's mountain, so there was only a handrail and a long, long drop separating us from the rolling valleys below. The sunshine was beautiful, coming down in rays of light and filtering through the trees with patterns like a kaleidoscope.

Up ahead, Savannah and Melissa laughed as they pedalled as fast as they could, trying to race each other. Lewis kept a steady pace behind them. Alex was just gliding along, not far behind me. I was only going slow because I was enjoying the views.

We passed under a bridge that had been decorated in colourful graffiti, then began our descent down a slope. I slowed up on the pedals. Ryan, ever the thrill seeker, only pedalled faster and went flying ahead of everyone. Even Savannah and Melissa had the sense to ease off a bit.

"Ryan, be careful!" I called, suddenly anxious. I mean, it was a pretty steep slope. If he lost control he'd go head first over the railing and that would be the end of him.

"Live a little, Aubs!" he called back, which made me groan in annoyance. I headed down after him, knowing I'd probably have to save his ass in a minute. When he reached the bottom, he pumped the brakes, and turned back to grin at me like a child. I rolled my eyes at him.

Gliding past Savannah and Melissa, I was fast approaching him. I hit the brakes, but they suddenly weren't working. My eyes widened.

"Oh, God," I groaned. Of *course* this was going to happen. Just my luck! I tried to use my foot against the pavement to slow down, but I was going so fast it didn't help much and seemed more dangerous than using the brakes themselves. I clamped onto the handbrake desperately. My body jerked, and felt myself go flying off the bike.

"Aubany!" Ryan cried, lunging forward.

I landed a few feet away, skidding along the concrete. The bike had fallen to its side and slid down after me, but before it could hit me Ryan had reached out to grab it by its back wheel. Melissa and Savannah cried out in alarm, dismounting to race down and check on me.

"Are you alright?" Ryan asked, looking concerned. I sat up and groaned, looking at the scrapes on my arms.

"Just a little banged up, but otherwise fine," I grimaced. "You *idiot!*"

I whacked him on the shoulder, and he looked honestly ashamed of himself.

"Come on," Ryan offered me his hand, and helped me to my feet. Savannah rubbed my back, looking worried, and Melissa inspected my scrapes.

"*Yeowch,*" she commented, but otherwise she seemed more amused at the whole situation.

I went to pick up my bike, but then noticed Alex had crouched beside it and was inspecting it.

"The brakes have been tampered with," Alex informed us, and my jaw dropped.

"Seriously?" I gasped. "That's so bad! Someone could sue the shop for that!"

"We *should,*" Ryan replied, looking angered now. I put a hand on his arm to calm him and shook my head.

"We *won't,* because I'm not a mean person," I corrected him. "I'm sure the shopkeeper had no intention of harming his customers. Unless he *wanted* to get sued, which I doubt. Whoever did this was probably a hooligan or someone who had nothing better to do. We'll just let the guy know not to rent this one out and to check all his other bikes."

"He should be checking them to begin with," Ryan muttered, but I ignored him. He was only upset because I'd gotten hurt. Overprotective wasn't a good look on him.

I wasn't planning on riding my tampered bike anymore, and we were a long way away from the town. There was still a fair way to the end of the track, too, and everyone was pretty keen to keep going. So when I told them to go on without me, Ryan immediately offered to go with me.

"She'll be fine, Ryan," Lewis commented. "You don't need to babysit her."

Ryan frowned at him, but I wasn't about to argue because he had a fair point. Not that I would have *minded,* but Ryan was acting pretty protective at the moment, and there was no need for him to give up going with the others to escort me back.

"It'll be fine, Ryan," I said. "I'll grab another bike and I'll catch up with you all."

"Are you sure?" Ryan asked, looking hesitant. I gave him a look that said *seriously?* That seemed to snap him out of it.

"Right. Well…I'll see you later, then," he said, before mounting his bike with the others. They all pedalled away, and I was then faced with the task of pushing my bike back up the steep hill on which I'd almost died not even two minutes ago.

CHAPTER ELEVEN

THE SNAP

Ryan's POV

When we arrived at the lookout, my anger had subsided…mostly. But it was taking all my strength to refrain from letting Lewis and his words get to me.

Just who did he think he was, anyway?

I knew Aubany could take care of herself. It was something I admired about her. She had more strength than she realized. But I'd only intended to look out for her. Plus, I was always wanting alone time with her. Especially since our time together might have been shorter than either of us realized.

Last night had certainly not helped me make a decision in any way. I kept having flashbacks that left me smiling to myself. Why would I ever want to part with someone who loved me so beautifully? Every touch…every kiss…and every meaning behind each action. She had only pure intentions, and I knew that. I knew her well enough to trust her by that.

I kept remembering everything I loved about us--everything I'd *miss* about us. Seeing her open up to me when we first fell in love was the most wonderful feeling. Her hot temper had simmered to a playful banter. Once communication with her had become bearable, it was like wiping a thick layer of dust off a beautiful treasure that you'd mistaken for a rock. Only it was so beautiful you couldn't part with it, no matter how much it was worth.

She was too good for me. That much I knew.

"Ryan?"

I was jolted from my thoughts when Lewis appeared at my side. I bit back a groan of annoyance.

"I didn't upset you earlier, did I?" he asked, looking cautious. I shrugged, not trusting myself to speak.

"Listen…I get it," Lewis said. He leaned on the handrail, looking out into the valley below us. "I worry about Melissa too, sometimes. But she's her own person—and I feel like you suffocate Aubany sometimes."

"What?" I snapped. He held up his hands in protest.

"I'm just saying—I know what you both went through on Nula Island. And I won't try to pretend like I get it. But I *do* know that Aubany can't move on from it if she can't even look out for herself. You're not helping her by trying to shelter her from the world."

"What makes you think that's what I'm doing?" I seethed. When had I *ever* given him that impression?

"You're always at her side," he pointed out. "She couldn't even cross that bridge on the hike without practically clinging to you."

I gritted my teeth, glaring at him.

"Look, I've just been doing some observing, is all, and I actually overheard you and Savannah last night. I know it's none of my business, but I think you'd be doing the right thing to break up with her."

Something snapped inside of me, and I punched him in the face. The impact sent pain through my knuckles.

"Ryan!" Melissa shrieked, dropping her bike and racing over. Before I could land another blow, Alex's hands were on me, pulling me back. Lewis held a hand to his bruised eye.

"What the *fuck,* Ryan?!" Melissa shouted, eyes burning with loathing as she glared at me. Savannah stepped in, trying to mediate the situation with her hands up between us.

"Come on—let's go," Alex said, trying to steer me away from them. My heart was pounding and blood roared in my ears, but the whole scene was a blur as I stormed back towards the bike track.

The plan had been to wait for Aubany to meet us here, but I was going back. I couldn't stay here.

"Would you like me to come with you?" Alex asked, but I shook my head.

"Thanks, but no," I grumbled, and left him behind as I went on ahead.

About fifteen minutes later, the anger was finally subsiding. My knuckles throbbed with dull pain and a feeling of hopelessness had come over me. Regardless of what Lewis had said and how he'd said it, he was right about one thing.

I *did* need to break up with Aubany. It just wasn't fair to her, and after last night it was more evident than ever that she loved me deeply. There was no way to do this without breaking her heart, but at least I could spare her from the pain later on.

Despite the difficultness of the realization, a light feeling came over me from having made my mind up. Like a weight had been lifted from my chest—except there was still one more weight to lift, and that one would be the hardest to face.

I was about halfway along the track when I noticed two other bike riders huddled around something on the ground up ahead, their bikes abandoned off to the side. They were blocking the entire path.

"Excuse me," I called out, interrupting the couple and making them look up. "Can I get past?"

"Oh, yeah," the man said, looking sheepish as he stood. "Just be careful—there's a girl here and she's unconscious."

He stepped out of the way, but the lady stayed where she was next to the girl. I suddenly had a clearer view of the scene, and I recognized the red strands of hair.

My heart plummeted and I raced over to Aubany's limp body.

"Aubs!" I cried, dropping to my knees. "What happened?"

"Do you know her?" the woman asked, looking shocked. "Oh, thank *God!* We called an ambulance and they're on their way, but we came across her when we were cycling. She was passed out and someone was trying to drag her off."

"What?" I asked, frowning in alarm. "Who?"

"Some girl. She seemed sort of familiar, actually, but I couldn't tell you who she was. Not off the top of my head."

"Where did she go?" I demanded.

The woman pointed towards the forest. "That way. She bolted and never came back. Not sure what she was trying to do with your friend here, but she didn't seem to be handling her very gently."

"What did she look like?" I pressed, a horrible feeling spreading through my chest.

"Um...brown hair? Kind of slim? She was wearing a green jacket."

Sheer dread came over me. It had to be Courtney. It *had* to be.

I couldn't believe I'd let Lewis talk me out of going with her. I couldn't believe I'd left her alone—if these people hadn't come along.....

I let out a long breath and buried my head in my hands, processing the whole situation. A mix of dread and relief swept through me all at once.

"We need to call the police," I said finally. "*Now.*"

A shiver went down my spine with how conveniently this had played out—Aubany's bike had been tampered with, which resulted in her getting separated from the rest of us. What a perfect opportunity for her to be snatched up!

I couldn't believe that, after all this time, Courtney had shown up again. *Here,* of all places!

I stepped back to call the police, and then I called Savannah to tell her what had happened. They told me they were on their way, and they arrived quickly on the bikes, hurrying to my side.

"Oh, my God," Melissa breathed, collapsing beside me. "Is she okay?"

She seemed to have momentarily forgotten about the incident with Lewis earlier, abandoning her anger towards me.

"I don't know," I replied hollowly.

The paramedics arrived before the police did, having been notified a lot earlier, and they did a basic check over Aubany. They were able to determine that she was hit over the head with an object of some kind, and she might have a concussion when she woke up.

"We'd like to monitor her for the rest of the day," one of the paramedics told us, as they lifted her into a stretcher. As they did, Aubany groaned and opened her eyes.

I was already at her side.

"Hey," I greeted, cupping her cheek. "How are you feeling?"

She groaned, and reached up to where she'd been hit.

"Easy," I said, folding my fingers around her arm. "You were knocked out. Do you remember what happened?"

She paused for a moment, trying to think.

"I don't really remember much," she admitted finally. "I feel like there's a huge chunk of memory missing."

"You likely do have memory missing," one of the paramedics explained. "Could be a concussion."

"I remember something coming out of nowhere to my right," she continued, clutching her head. "I think I was hit, but I can't say for sure because I don't remember *being* hit. The next thing I remember is waking up here."

"So, you didn't see *who* hit you?" the police officer asked her, scribbling all the information down on a notepad. She shook her head.

"No. It was just *something* coming at me. It was so fast—and I didn't get a good look. Or maybe I did. Like I said, I don't remember."

The police informed us that they were going to contact the team investigating the Courtney Madsen case and tell them they might have a suspected lead. Our parents were going to be notified, which was inevitable.

The paramedics informed us they were taking Aubany after that, so I told her we'd meet her at the hospital afterwards. After they'd left, the police scoped out the area of the incident, taking reports from all of us on what had happened.

They sent two people out to investigate the bike shop and the tampering, in case it turned out to be linked. But apart from that, there was nothing more to be done.

"You kids should pack up and head home," the police officer said as he was preparing to leave. "With someone like this on your trail, it's not safe to be out here. We'll do everything we can to find this person, but we can't guarantee your safety if you're not in a secured area. In the meantime, if your friend remembers anything else, get her to ring this number."

He handed us a card. We all nodded and thanked them for their help, and they headed off. The other strangers headed off too, and we exchanged our thanks to them as well. There was a moment of grave silence as we stood there, coming to terms with what had happened.

I turned to the others. "We should probably get back and start packing up, then," I said.

The others nodded in agreement—well, everyone except Lewis, who was still sulking in the background with his now black eye.

Alex had bought my bike back with him after I'd stormed off earlier—and I was thankful now, because it was faster to ride our bikes back to the shop. The hairs on the back of my neck rose every time I glanced around at the pine trees lining the bike path.

Courtney was still out here somewhere. She could be hiding *anywhere*. She could even be watching us right now.

~

I was returning my bike to the store employee inside the shop when the sound of Melissa cursing loudly from the parking lot drew my attention. From beside me, Alex dropped his own bike. It clattered against the counter as we rushed out to investigate.

Melissa was standing beside the Ute, gripping her hair as she inspected the tires. My gaze travelled down to see that they had been slashed.

"You're joking," Alex muttered from beside me.

"And that's not all!" Savannah called from the window of her own car—a small hatchback. Her tires appeared to be slashed too, but she was in the driver's seat fiddling with the ignition. It made a strange, spluttering sound, but refused to start.

"I think our engines have been tampered with too," she explained, poking her head back out.

Dread was slowly spreading through every inch of my body again.

This had been intentional—of *course* it had been. Courtney wanted to keep us here as long as she could. Now, we would have to find a mechanic, and likely wire money from our parents to have *both* sets of tires replaced and *both* engines fixed. Either that, or....

"Is there a bus that goes from here?" Melissa asked, running a hand through her hair as she let out a steady breath and began pacing. "A bus, or a train, or *something....*"

"We can't just leave the cars here," Lewis said, speaking for the first time since we'd found Aubany unconscious. He'd been standing back watching us as we reacted to the cars. "Even if we did leave, we'd have to come back for the cars—and someone would need to stay behind to ensure they get fixed."

"Are you volunteering?" Alex asked, his tone even but his expression challenging as he folded his arms. "Because there is no way Sav and I are staying here with that lunatic running around."

Savannah nodded in agreement. Her face was slightly pale, and I didn't blame her. I, too, was not keen to stay here a moment longer than necessary.

"Look, let's just talk to a mechanic. Maybe it's something they can fix today, and then we can leave."

We contemplated for a moment, and then Melissa let out a reluctant sigh.

"Alright," she said. "But while we do that, some-one should go check on Aubany."

To my surprise, her eyes fell on me. I would have thought that she would be the one to volunteer, being her best friend and all—but then I saw the loathing in her eyes and remembered that I'd punched Lewis earlier. She probably didn't want me around him.

"Good call," I replied shortly. "Savannah, will you come with me? I figure it's better to stay in pairs than go anywhere alone right now."

"Of course," she said, hurrying over to my side. "We'll text you when we get there, and we'll meet you guys back at the cabin or something."

They nodded in agreement, and we parted ways.

CHAPTER TWELVE

SECRET LOVER

Aubany's POV

A slow beep had become music in my ears as I lay in a hospital bed.

The nurses had given me some painkillers for my throbbing head, but apart from that I felt okay. Banged up and shaken, but okay. I was relieved to have nurses and people passing by regularly, even if I didn't have my full privacy. There had been no spare rooms, so they'd set me up in a wing with only a curtain for separation to the other patients around.

I was relieved to see Ryan walk in when he did— and accompanied by Savannah.

"You guys," I breathed, and Ryan came to wrap his warm arm carefully around me.

"How are you feeling?" he asked me, his blue eyes burning with concern as he sat on the edge of my bed. Savannah perched on my other side.

"I'm fine. Apart from my forehead—but I guess that's to be expected, considering I got whacked in the head. Bits and pieces are coming back to me...I remember seeing a pipe...but it's not enough to confirm if it was Courtney."

"But there's no doubt that it was her," Savannah said quickly. "Who *else* could it have been?"

"Right," Ryan agreed, nodding. "I'm just glad we found you when we did. I can't imagine what would have happened…."

He trailed off, avoiding my gaze, and I reached out to entwine my fingers with his. It wasn't his fault.

"Are we going home?" I asked. "Because I've been thinking—what if Courtney follows us? What if we lead her right to the doorstep of our homes?"

The very prospect filled me with an intense fear that made my gut twist uncomfortably.

"Well, I still think we'd be safer in our own homes," Savannah said firmly. "At least there are more witnesses in our neighbourhoods. But the cabin? It's completely secluded from the town!"

"I agree," I said quickly. "But I don't like the idea of her knowing about the one place I feel safe at."

Savannah grimaced, seeming to hesitate for a moment, but then spoke,

"Aubany, I don't want to be the one to say this...but if she managed to find us here, I'm fairly sure she knows where you live already."

My face must have gone pale, because she quickly added,

"I mean, she was probably just waiting for the right moment. You were isolated, away from home...no one was around. Imagine how easy it would have been to make you disappear here, compared to in your hometown. The difference is that she *can't* touch you in your hometown—there are too many people looking out for you."

I began to shake, and Ryan shot her a look that told her to stop talking.

"Aubs," he said gently, reaching to stroke my back soothingly. "I'm not going to let anything happen to you, okay? You're safe as long as I'm around. And lucky for you, I just happen to be your neighbour, so all you have to do is scream and I'll be over in seconds to help you."

I imagined such a scene playing out and the whole thing seemed preposterous. Still, his words reassured me slightly, and I leaned into his touch.

"But..." Ryan said, his expression changing, and a feeling of dread came over me again. "As it turns out, we *can't* leave yet, because Courtney tampered with our cars. We may have to stay here a while longer."

It took me a second to process what he'd said.

We *couldn't* leave.

That was no longer an option.

"Unless," he said firmly, using his other hand to squeeze mine, "we found a bus or train to take us back—and all you have to do is say the word and I'll be getting on it with you. I'm not leaving you on your own until I know you're safe."

Did I *want* that?

I honestly didn't know. I didn't feel safe no matter *where* I went, and leaving the others behind didn't make me feel better. How would I know *they* were safe if I just left them to go back home?

I couldn't do that.

"When are they discharging you?" Savannah asked, swiftly changing the subject.

"Later today," I replied. "As long as my condition remains stable, that is."

"Well, you have a bit of time to decide what you want to do, then," she said soothingly. "And by then, we should know what the situation is with the cars. For all we know, we may be able to leave as soon as tomorrow morning."

I nodded, relishing in the thought. I wanted to go—but not without the others. And not without certainty that I would be safe. Somehow, I felt safer in our own cars than travelling on public transport.

"Do you want me to stay with you?" Ryan asked, and I nodded. I squeezed his hand a little tighter, afraid he would let go—but he didn't.

"Okay. I'll stay," he promised me, tucking a strand of my hair behind my ear. "Everything's going to be fine—I swear it."

~

It was roughly an hour later, when Ryan and Savannah had gone to find some lunch from the hospital cafeteria, that my mom rang. I'd been expecting as much, but nothing had prepared me for the phone call.

I clicked answer.

"Hey, Mom," I said.

"Oh, *Aubany!"* she breathed, and I could hear the worry in her voice. "I'm so glad you're okay—the police were just here. They got a call about Courtney and came to talk to us. You need to come home—"

"I can't," I said quickly. "Courtney slashed all our car tires."

There was a moment of silence. I heard a tremble in her voice as she spoke,

"What?"

I sighed.

"Yeah. I'm still in the hospital. They'll probably let me go this afternoon. Ryan and Savannah and here with me. But they told me they got back from the bike ride we were on and found their cars like that. They're already in with a mechanic, but we don't know how long it's going to take to fix yet."

"Well, then I'll send your father," she insisted. "He'll come get you."

"Mom," I said firmly. "I know you're worried. I am too—believe me, the last thing I want is to be here right now. But there are six of us, and I can't leave the others behind to fend for themselves."

"Aubany, I don't want you there all alone—"

"I'm not alone," I reminded her. "Ryan's with me. He protected me for *six weeks* last time."

"Aubany."

My mom's voice was stern, but there was a pause. I took the opportunity to continue,

"You're going to have to send two people if you come get us. And then you'll have to come *back* to pick up the cars. It's not worth it."

"Nothing is more important than your life," Mom whispered back.

"Look," I said pointedly. "We're not stupid. We're not going to continue on here like nothing has happened. Just...let me find out about the cars first. I'll ring you back to let you know when they'll be ready to go. And as soon as we can leave, we will."

Another pause. I could tell she was unhappy about this.

"I *promise* we'll be careful. We'll do everything in our power to protect ourselves."

It was a few more seconds before I heard a relenting sigh on the other end.

"Fine," she said. "But if it's going to take longer than a few days, I don't care. I'm sending someone to get you—and even if it's just you who comes back, I'll see to it that they collect you."

"Understood," I replied, and I knew she was dead serious.

She begged me to be extra careful before hanging up, and I let my head fall back against the pillows. It would have been so easy to let her come get me...but I could never do that to my friends.

I wouldn't leave them to go through what I went through last time.

~

I was discharged later that day, and as we were walking out of the hospital, Ryan's phone rang.

"It's Alex," he said, before answering it and bringing it up to his ear. "Yeah?"

They spoke for a few moments, but I couldn't gauge what the verdict was until the conversation had finished and Ryan turned to Savannah and I.

"So, the mechanic can fix the Ute by tomorrow—but the repair shop needs to order in the parts for Savannah's car, and they won't get here for another day or two. As for the tires, they're being replaced as we speak."

We grimaced.

"So, what does that mean?" Savannah asked wearily, wrapping her arms around her torso and shifting her weight uncomfortably.

"Well, apparently Lewis wants to wait until the parts arrive before we leave. He thinks it'll be easier that way. It *is* only a couple of days."

Somehow, I felt like waiting was a terrible idea. But the alternative was leaving someone behind—likely Savannah, because it was her car we were waiting on. If Courtney was still around, Savannah was more likely to be targeted than Melissa or Lewis, because she was the only other person Courtney knew from Nula Island.

"Then we'll just have to wait it out," I said finally, though it came out more like a breath. "I don't want us splitting up. I'll need to call my Mom and tell her."

Ryan studied my expression, but nodded.

"Okay. Well, let's head back to the cabin and we can figure out our next steps."

By the time we had walked back, my legs were aching from the long walk—and the others were already gathered in the living room with a fire crackling lazily. Their gazes turned to us as we walked in the front door.

"Good, you're back," Melissa said.

I glanced at Lewis, who was standing near her. He had a swollen, black eye, and my stomach lurched. Had Courtney struck again?

"What happened?" I exclaimed, rushing forward.

Momentarily, the group exchanged confused glances, but then a realization seemed to come over them.

"Oh," Alex said. "Ah—"

"Ryan punched Lewis earlier," Melissa cut in shortly, folding her arms and glaring at him.

What?

I turned to Ryan, my mouth falling open with shock. That was so unlike him!

He came up beside me, and I noticed how tense his shoulders were as he bluntly chipped in,

"He deserved it."

I glanced back and forth between the two, trying to piece together what had happened, but Savannah stepped in before the tension snapped between them.

"You guys, we can't afford to be fighting," she said firmly. "We need to secure the cabin so that Courtney can't get in here. We should decide on one door to use for entry into the house, and keep the rest locked. The windows, too. And we should block off all the windows on the lower floor with what we can find."

Lewis frowned at the idea of his cabin being re-arranged, but the rest of us were adamant about the idea. We broke off and began checking all the locks, while the boys started heaving bookcases and chairs to press firmly against the windows.

Once we'd finished, we all collapsed in the lounge room. My forehead was beaded with sweat, and it was beginning to get dark.

"We should get dinner started," Alex said after a moment. "I know how to cook a really nice chicken soup. It'll be quick and easy."

"Yes...except we don't have any chicken stock," Melissa replied, frowning.

Lewis sat up straighter.

"I'll go into town and get some," he said. I raised my eyebrows at him.

"Alone?" I asked. "No. Take someone with you."

"I'll be fine," replied. "Courtney's targeting you guys, right? She probably doesn't even know who I am—or Melissa, for that matter. I won't be long."

"Lewis, that's insane," Melissa protested, her expression furrowing with worry now. She reached out to grab his hand as he stood, but he waved her off.

"Relax," he replied, kissing her forehead before stepping around her armchair to head for the door. My gaze followed him, and I narrowed my eyes.

Something felt *off*.

I remembered, all of a sudden, about the strange phone call incident in the bathroom earlier that day. I'd *completely* forgotten with all the other events going on.

A sudden rush came over me, mixed with dread as I realized that I had to go after him. He was probably using this opportunity to meet up with his mystery hook-up girl! But that meant venturing outside, into the dark woods with the likes of Courtney slinking around.

Not appealing.

I must have been making a strange face, because a hand suddenly covered mine. My head whipped back around to find Ryan giving me a questioning look.

My fingernails dug into the armchair.

"I have to go to the bathroom," I muttered, and quickly jumped up to hurry down the hall. Once I was out of their view, I snuck around to the kitchen. We'd threaded all the keys to the house onto a single keychain and left it in the fruit bowl on the counter for safekeeping. Now, I very carefully edged the keychain out, praying silently it wouldn't jingle and draw attention. It made the tiniest, slow-drawn scraping noise against the ceramic bowl.

My eyes flickered towards the living room, but nobody had stirred.

When I'd coaxed it far enough out, my fingers snapped against the keys on the chain to stop them from clinking and I hurried to the back door. Very slowly and quietly, I slid the key in and turned until I heard a click.

I held my breath, and glanced over my shoulder. The others were still oblivious.

I slipped out the back door and quietly shut it, before tearing around the house to catch up with Lewis.

When I reached the front of the house, I kept my-self low and slowed my pace on the gravel to avoid alerting anyone of my presence. I spotted Lewis miles up the driveway, walking in almost complete darkness save for the moonlight illuminating the way.

He seemed to be holding his phone to his ear, and I could hear his faint voice talking.

Gritting my teeth, I crept through the grass towards the trees lining the driveway, then kept myself on the edge of the tree line as I followed behind him.

"I'm doing everything I can," I heard him say. A pause, and then, "I know you need us to stay, but it will look suspicious if I try to convince them while they're in danger. We need a new plan."

Another pause, and I strained to listen while maintaining my distance. It suddenly occurred to me that I should be filming all of this as evidence for Melissa. I whipped out my phone, and the light blinded me. Lewis slowed his pace.

Shit!

I lunged behind a tree trunk and shut the phone off quickly, taking short breaths. Had he seen me? Had the light alerted him?

I waited, and then I heard him say,

"Look, I can try—but they're not likely to leave the cabin now. It's going to be hard for you to sneak in and out."

Sneak in and out? But how? Surely this girl would be noticed by one of us...

The locked room, I realized.

This girl Lewis was seeing was using the locked room to sneak in and out! But *how?* It was so high up. Was she using a ladder or something?

At that moment, another realization hit me—if the room was locked from the inside, and the window was unlocked, that meant Courtney had a way in and out. If she could find a way up to that window, she could get in—and *none* of us could stop her unless we put a chair to the door or something.

My mind was whirling with all of these realizations, and I became vaguely aware of Lewis' footsteps crunching away from me again. I didn't realize I was gripping my phone so hard until I felt the sweat begin to bead on my palm.

"I'll think of something," I heard Lewis say, more faintly. "I love you too."

The words slammed into me. *Confirmation.*

So he *did* have some secret lover out here. Was it an old summer fling? Some girl he'd known growing up?

I gritted my teeth, and my heart ached for Melissa. She was going to be devastated when she found out—but she deserved to know the truth.

Speaking of which, I didn't have any recorded evidence—but if I could catch this girl in the act of sneaking in, I'd be golden.

A surge of determination swept through me, and I took a step forward towards the cabin.

Two strong arms gripped my shoulders from behind and slammed me back against the tree. I gasped, and my heart thudded as Lewis side-stepped around me into view, one hand pressing me against the tree trunk, the other twirling his phone.

"Going somewhere?" he asked slyly.

CHAPTER THIRTEEN

THE LOCKED BEDROOM

Aubany's POV

"What did you hear just now?" he asked me, his voice frightfully dark. Dread like oil seeped through every bone in my body.

"Enough," I managed to grind out, but my unsteady breaths gave my fear away. "Let me go, Lewis."

"I don't think so," he replied evenly. "You should have stayed back in the cabin."

Despite his chilling words, my temper flared more than my fear as I narrowed my gaze.

"*You* should have covered your tracks better—I know about your side girl, Lewis. I caught her in the bathroom this morning."

He frowned, cocking his head slightly.

"You *caught* her?" he repeated slowly.

I let out a shaky, relenting breath.

"Okay...not *caught* her—I walked in on her. But I hid. She didn't know I was there. And I didn't see anything! I'm not a pervert. I saw the caller ID on her phone—*your* ID."

He stared at me for a moment before releasing my shoulders and taking a slow step back from me.

"What do *you* think's going on?" he asked me carefully.

I rolled my eyes. "Don't play games with me, Lewis—it's pretty *obvious* what's going on! You're *cheating* on Melissa! I heard you say *I love you* to some other girl—do you say that to all your girls? Are there more Melissa doesn't know about?"

He burst out laughing, and my blood boiled even more. It took him a moment to stop, and there was an expression like relief on his face.

"Oh, Aubany," he chuckled, pressing his hand against his forehead as he shook his head. "Yes...*yes, that's what's going on."

Something about his tone seemed off, but I couldn't place what it was. Either way, he was still an asshole.

"Could you be any more insensitive?" I cried angrily, watching his every reaction. "No wonder Ryan punched you earlier—I bet you *did* deserve it!"

That seemed to bring him back to his senses, and all the laughter vanished from the air.

"Sure. If that's what will make you feel better about your boyfriend punching someone, go ahead and think that," he drawled slowly. "But if I'm an ass-hole for what I'm doing, then he's an asshole, too, for what he's been doing to *you.*"

What?

He smirked at the sight of my stunned expression. Anger flared again, and I shook off his words.

"You're just trying to cause drama between us. Ryan would *never* do anything to hurt me."

"He already has," Lewis replied, his voice low. "You just don't realize it yet."

"And how would you know?" I challenged, clenching my fists.

"Because he *punched* me when I told him to do the right thing by you," he said bluntly, his eyes boring into mine. A coldness came over me—because *that* I couldn't deny. I didn't even know why Ryan had punched Lewis. But now I was afraid to ask...and yet, I couldn't get the thought out of my head.

And the more I thought about it, the more it made sense. Ryan wasn't the violent type. Even on Nula Island, he had gone with Courtney and put himself in danger to save me, rather than straight out attack her. For him to punch someone, Lewis would have had to have hit a *huge* nerve.

What was he hiding from me?

"I suggest you worry about your own relationship before you go poking around in mine," Lewis drawled slowly, seeming to relish in the way I'd shrunk back with crestfallen eyes. I could tell he thought he'd won, because with a smug smile, he stepped past me and began walking up the driveway again.

The chicken soup, I remembered.

I could only just bring myself to walk back to the cabin, the forbidding fear in my heart numbing to a bearable, dull ache.

~

When I returned, I slipped back in the way I had gone, but then curled up behind the counter in the kitchen.

I suddenly wasn't so sure that Melissa would want to hear the truth—because I didn't know if *I* could bear to hear it about Ryan. And if Melissa loved Lewis the way I loved Ryan....

Almost by a cruel twist of fate, it was Melissa who found me there half an hour later. She nearly tripped over me on her way to the fridge.

"Aubany!" she cried, clutching a hand to her chest. "What the hell are you doing down there?"

Then she noticed my expression, and she immediately knelt to join me on the floor.

"What happened?" she asked, more quietly.

"Where is everyone?" I asked, worried about being overheard.

"They're playing cards," she told me. "I didn't know you were here, though—I thought you were constipated in the bathroom or something."

Great. If I didn't know better, Ryan was probably sitting outside the toilet door, strumming away and trying to and soothe me when I wasn't even *in* there!

The thought nearly made me smile—expect Lewis' words still echoed in my head, and it only lifted the tension enough for me to say what I'd been wanting to say to Melissa all day.

"Lewis is cheating on you."

Melissa's expression fell, and she slowly leaned back from me. Her mouth opened, but no words came out.

I knew what she wanted to say. She wanted to deny it, to ask me if this was a joke, to ask me how I could dare to accuse him of such a thing.

But I was her best friend since childhood, and she knew I'd never say something like this unless it were true.

"I found out this morning...and he confirmed it this evening," I explained gently. "I wasn't in the bathroom. I tailed him."

Tears welled in her eyes. She blinked them away and wiped them on her sleeve, but they kept coming. Lines of anger appeared in her brow when they kept coming, and she buried her face in both hands to hide it.

"Are you sure?" I heard her ask, muffled by her hands.

My own eyes began to string, and I placed a gentle hand on her shoulder.

"He said *I love you* to her."

There was a moment of silence, before a muffled sob escaped her lips. I hadn't been aware of the low murmur coming from the living room until Melissa's next sob came out strangled, and the murmurs ceased.

Suddenly, the loud sobs were echoing off the walls, and everyone was rushing to crowd into the kitchen. I was silently cursing for having done this here.

"What happened?" Savannah asked, leaning around the counter.

"Get out," Melissa choked violently. Savannah sprang back, and I knew it was time to go. I quickly stood and placed a hand on Savannah's arm to indicate that she should move.

Alex stepped towards Melissa.

"Melis—"

"Get out!" she demanded, ripping her tearstained face away from her hands.

Lewis wasn't back yet. But I had a feeling a storm was about to go down the moment he stepped in.

Quickly, I urged for Savannah and the others to leave Melissa and steered us all out of the kitchen.

~

The yelling started downstairs when we heard Lewis return through the back door.

It was muffled, but it was enough to keep me awake as I lay in bed. Ryan had snuck to the bathroom to take a long shower, and I was glad—I didn't know if I could face him right now.

My heart beat wildly at the thought of confronting him. My head simply couldn't process the concept that he would hurt me in any way. He wouldn't *do* that to me.

Would he?

The room was dark, and when the door creaked open, light spilled in from the hallway. I rolled over in the bed so I wouldn't be facing him when he flicked the lights on and shut the door.

"Aubs, you awake?" he asked, crossing the room. I kept my eyes closed and focused on slowing my breathing, hoping he would think I was asleep. A few moments of silence passed, and I couldn't hear any movement in the room. I strained to listen for foot-steps, rustling of clothes...*anything*.

Eventually, the curiosity consumed me and I opened my eyes. He was standing by the dresser, staring at the mirror with his shirtless back to me.

I frowned, and his agonized gaze caught mine in the reflection. The guilt in his eyes instantly vanished.

A coldness came over my heart as he turned to me and gave me a soft smile.

No....

How easily he had masked his deception, in the mere blink of an eye.

Why had I trusted him? How could I let myself fall so deep that I became oblivious to the idea that he could *still* trick me? Why had I been so *stupid* to believe this could last forever? That guys like Ryan could be with girls like me? Maybe for a short while—but of *course* he'd get sick of me.

Somehow, it hurt even more now—because I hadn't been guarded these past seven months. I'd completely let my walls down to Ryan. I'd *believed* in him more than anyone else in my life.

But Lewis had been right—there was someone else.

"I didn't think you'd be able to sleep," he said, giving me a knowing look as the sounds of Melissa and Lewis shouting downstairs continued to ricochet through the floorboards.

But I wasn't focused on that—because the guilt in Ryan's eyes was replaying in my head on a loop. I felt like a numbness had spread over every inch of my body.

Ryan came to laze on the bed beside me.

"What happened down there?" he asked me, his eyes filled with concern now. He reached out to tuck a strand of my red hair behind my ear, and I felt tears well in my eyes.

Alarmed, Ryan jerked back.

"What's wrong?" he asked, sitting up straighter now. I blinked the tears away and ducked my head. The words I wanted to ask were stuck in my throat.

"It's nothing. Let's just go to bed," I said, turning away from him. My fingers clung to the sheets like a cocoon that could protect me from Ryan as he went to turn out the light—but I knew nothing could protect me from what I felt for him.

My love for him was like a forest—so deep you could get lost in it forever. And like a winter chill steals all the leaves from the branches, that love was leaving me bare and vulnerable enough to cut me down and leave me bleeding.

I didn't know if I could stand to get my heart broken. It wouldn't be like last time—when I'd been in love with Ryan for a minute and had made up with him within a day. This was *months* of my life, *wasted* on something I'd believed in...*someone* I'd believed in.

Ryan didn't reach out to touch me or hug me like he usually did. We kept our space, and I let silent tears streak down my cheeks as sleep overtook me.

~

I woke early that morning from tortured dreams, a strange ache in my heart. It was still dark outside, but the sun was rising.

I couldn't stand to be in bed with Ryan any longer, so I quietly got up, pulled on a warm sweater and jeans, and snuck downstairs. The floorboards were icy beneath my feet and I shivered, cursing that I'd forgotten my socks. But I wasn't going back up there, so I found my boots by the door and put those on instead.

They made a heavy, echoing *thump* every time I walked, and I prayed I wouldn't wake the whole house up as I crept as quietly as I could towards the kitchen.

Melissa and Lewis were gone—probably asleep, though I wasn't sure where. The couch was empty, but I doubted they would have shared a room after last night. Maybe one of them had left...or maybe Lewis was in the out-of-bounds bedroom.

As I reached for a mug and packet of instant coffee on the counter, my gaze turned upward towards the ceiling. The out-of-bounds bedroom was right above me.

Narrowing my gaze, I looked out the kitchen window. The cabin was built on stilts around the side, past the back door, and the ground sloped down slightly towards the lake on that side. If there was a way up, you'd definitely need a ladder or something.

I frowned for a moment, my hands resting gently on the mug I'd grabbed, before I whirled around to head for the back door.

Coming face to face with Ryan. My heart stopped and I gasped.

"Jesus!" I breathed, clutching a hand to my chest. "Don't *do* that, Ryan!"

He frowned just a little.

"Sorry," he replied, reaching for my hand and squeezing it. The gesture was reassuring—until I remembered last night, and suddenly my heart was torn between ripping my hand away and leaning into his touch.

"What are you doing up so early?" he asked. His gaze drifted to my boots and he added, "And why are you wearing those? You might as well have stuck rocks to your feet."

I bit my lip, because I couldn't tell him. Not without letting on that I didn't trust him anymore, which may hurt him—and it *sucked* that I still cared about his feelings more than my own.

He slowly stepped forward, and I got a whiff of the cedarwood soap he always used.

"If you wanted to wake me up, there are *much* better ways," he added huskily, reaching to wrap his arms around me.

I stepped back.

"Sorry, I just—I couldn't sleep," I babbled. "With Lewis...and *Courtney*...I'm feeling really on edge. I actually want to check around the house. Just to...make sure it's safe, you know?"

He frowned, watching my sporadic movements, before reaching to take both of my hands in his.

"Aubs, listen—I won't let any harm come to you," he promised, bringing my knuckles to his lips and kissing them. "You trust me, don't you?"

I froze, and he noticed. I saw a flash of hurt in his eyes and regret washed over me—but it was too late.

He let go of my hands and grimaced, sticking his hands into his pyjama pockets.

"Well, if you're really that unnerved, we can go take a look around."

I raised an eyebrow at him.

"Really?" I asked, and he nodded.

"Come on—let's do a round of the perimeter," he said, grabbing the keys from the fruit bowl.

I followed him to the back door, which he unlocked and stepped through. The air was even colder outside, and I rubbed my arms to try and stay warm.

"Shall we go this way?" he asked, stepping to the left, but I grabbed his arm to stop him.

"I want to look in the out-of-bounds room," I said firmly, and he cocked his head at me.

I took a deep breath. "I spoke to Lewis last night—that's how I found out he was cheating on Melissa. There's…a girl, and I *think* she's been sneaking in and out of that bedroom. But I don't know how, and it makes me nervous—because if it's true, that means Courtney can get in, and we wouldn't even know—"

"Woah, *woah.*"

Ryan lifted his hands to stop me on my tangent, then stepped forward to cup my cheeks.

"Okay, first of all—Lewis is a dick," he said, and I couldn't help but smirk despite my feelings towards him right now. "Second of all—do you realize how ridiculous that sounds? How the hell would anyone even get up there?"

"Well, maybe there's a ladder," I said, turning to peer under the cabin where the support beams stood.

"Did you see one when you grabbed the raft the other day?"

"Uh, I don't know—there's a lot of crap under there," Ryan replied, jerking his head to indicate.

He wasn't wrong. As we stepped through the dewy, morning grass to take a closer look, all I could make out was mismatched junk; old boat parts, a box of nails, some folding tables with rusted legs, a few tires--even the raft, which was now a deflated heap on the floor. We edged our way through it all until Ryan finally grabbed my arm and tugged.

"There," he pointed, and sure enough, there was a wooden ladder leaning against the wall, so dark it almost blended in amongst the chaotic mess.

Together, Ryan and I heaved it out, as it didn't fold up or bend, and with some strategic balancing (by which I mean I nearly toppled down the slope with it), we managed to lean it against the cabin wall so it met with the window to the out-of-bounds bed-room.

I huffed and wiped the sweat from my brow as I stood back to admire our handiwork.

"So, I suppose you have a fear of ladders, too," Ryan joked, smirking at me as he folded his arms. I gave a single, humourless chuckle back, and his ex-pression became serious.

"Do you want me to climb up and look for you?"

I shook my head, my eyes locked on the window.

"No," I replied, as resolve settled within me. "I need to see this for myself."

CHAPTER FOURTEEN

WHERE LOVE COMES TO DIE

Aubany's POV

My entire body shook with nerves as I climbed the final rung of the steep ladder. Ryan was at the bottom, holding it secure, but that didn't make me feel much better when my hands were so clammy and slippery from fear.

As the interior of the room came into view through the window, I squinted to make out everything in the dark. There was a dusty rug on the floor, a wooden post bed with a matching wardrobe, and faded pink sheets. Some ordinary flower paintings hung from the left wall, and in all honesty, it just looked like an old bedroom.

A *girl's* bedroom, in fact. Maybe it had been Lewis' sister's old room.

Maybe *that* was the real reason he hadn't wanted us to go in there.

I tried to open the window but it didn't budge, proving it was locked from the inside. Relief swept through me—and I determined from looking at it that it couldn't possibly be opened from the outside.

But my relief was short-lived, because if *that* were the case, then how was the girl Lewis had been seeing coming and going?

How had she been in the bathroom that one morning, yet come and gone without us knowing?

The hairs on the back of my neck stood up. It just didn't make sense.

"What do you see?" Ryan called.

"It looks normal," I called back, defeated. "Old, actually."

I began to descend the ladder, and when my feet touched the ground, I felt all the tension release from my arms from holding on. I turned to Ryan, whose hands immediately went to my shoulders to steady me.

"Were there any signs of damage?" Ryan asked.

"Not that I could tell," I replied, frowning. But then I realized why he was asking—Lewis had said the floorboards were damaged!

If that were the case, wouldn't we have noticed from the kitchen?

There was no damage in that room. Lewis had been lying for some reason...unless, again, it was merely because it was his sister's old room.

I felt like I wouldn't be settled on the matter until we had a key, but I doubted Lewis would give it to us. Let alone to *me,* of all people, and certainly not to Ryan after he had punched him.

Speaking of which....

"Ryan," I began, my heart beginning to thud again. "Why did you punch Lewis?"

He froze, his eyes staring at me wildly like he'd been caught in headlights.

"Is that what you've been upset about?" he asked.

"No!" I said quickly. "I mean, *yes*--I don't know—Lewis *said* something—"

"Lewis is a liar," Ryan cut in quickly. "We literally just established that."

His eyes darted and I knew he was panicking. Covering his tracks, trying to blow off my words--it sparked a nerve in me.

"What are you hiding from me, Ryan?" I blurted out before I could stop myself. Anger flared through me, and he faltered, the guilt returning to his eyes.

"Aubs, I'm not...."

"You *are*," I demanded, folding my arms. "You won't talk to me about the scholarship. You've got this *look* in your eyes right now, and you would *never* punch Lewis unless he said something to really trigger you. So what is it?"

He didn't answer. Tears welled in my eyes.

"Or, rather, *who* is it?" I added, feeling my lip quiver as those tears began to fall down my cheeks. His eyes widened and he reached to cup my cheeks again.

"No—no, no, no—Aubs, there's no one else—"

I tried to wriggle out of his grip but he wrapped his arms around me. He held me like that for a moment, swaying gently with me.

"Aubany, I'm sorry. I never meant to cause you to doubt me or mistrust me," he breathed in my ear. His arms around me was a comfort, and I *needed* it. I couldn't bear the thought of losing it, or losing *him*. My arms clung tighter around him. "I'm sorry I didn't talk to you about this. I...couldn't bring myself to hurt you."

His words pieced through my heart—because they basically confirmed what Lewis had said to me. I knew what was coming next couldn't be good, and swallowed hard.

He stepped back, and his breath was shaky. I'd never seen him look so visibly upset—his eyes seemed glassy.

"I haven't applied for the scholarship because...I was trying to decide between pursuing my music or staying with you."

It took a moment for his words to sink in. The logical part of me heard him, but the part that was crazy, deeply, *passionately* in love with him....

"What are you talking about?" I asked weakly. He let out a slow breath.

"I'm saying…we can't have it both ways. It's not fair on you."

My heart lurched. "No," I said quickly. "No—we *can.* Why would you think that?"

"Aubs, listen to me," he said, holding me gently by the shoulders. "I love you with all of my heart...and that is why I can't do this to you. I don't think you realize what it would be like for you if my music career takes off. How hard it would be for you to be on your own for months at a time—especially in a place like LA, where both of our paychecks would go a long way towards rent. It's not as easy as you think it's going to be, and I don't want you to plan your life around me. I want you to *live* it."

"But...but...." I stammered, hot tears rolling freely now. "I *love* you, Ryan—I thought we agreed we'd do this together! I want to be with you. I don't care how hard it is! We didn't survive Nula Island just to *not* be together!"

"But this is real life, Aubs," Ryan said gently, his own eyes filling with tears now. "It's just how it is."

Everything came to a stop, and I found myself pushing away from him, hard.

"Real life?" I cried. "This *is* my life—and it *is* real! Courtney is still *real,* Ryan. Nula Island wasn't some fantasy, or some dream. It happened, and you're telling me that after all of that—after all of *this"*—I gestured to the space between us, a representation of the months we'd spent together—

".—you just want to give up? Like it never happened? Like I didn't *risk my life* for you on that island and suffer a near-fatal *stab* wound?"

"Aubs," Ryan said, holding up his hands, but my blood simmered.

"You've got to be kidding me," I seethed at him. Hurt and betrayal slit through me like ice.

To my dismay, he made no attempt to mend the situation. In fact, he stepped back with a look of defeat. Almost as if he'd accepted this reality *long* before now, and was simply enduring how it was playing out.

I let out a staggered breath—something between a gasp and a huff, and my eyes began to sting again.

I was so stupid.

"*Screw you,* Ryan Rupert!" I turned on my heel and fled back inside. Hot tears spilled from my eyes in my desperation to get away, and the dewy soles of my boots left mud tracks on the kitchen floorboards as I thudded through the cabin.

When I reached the stairs I ran into Savannah, who was still rubbing the sleep from her eyes.

"Aubany?" she asked. She then noticed my tears and her eyes widened. "What happened?"

"I can't be here," I mumbled pushing past towards the front door. I couldn't be in this house, in this *space*—I couldn't even *look* at Ryan right now.

"Wait—let me come with you," Savannah insisted, reaching for my arm, but I shook my head.

"I need to be alone," I said, before stepping outside.

~

The tears falling before were nothing compared to the tears that came as soon as I was alone in the woods. I broke down into ugly sobs and collapsed, hugging my knees like my legs couldn't hold me up anymore.

The tears flowed. My breaths came out ragged and my heart hurt unlike anything I'd ever felt in my life. It came a close second to the stab wound I'd received on Nula Island, but it *felt* like Ryan had just stabbed me clean through my heart.

As I cried, I let myself curl up in the leaves. I stayed there for a long time—maybe an hour, maybe longer—and every time I thought I was done, I would think of another memory and it would start all over again, like a dam breaking.

I had *never* felt such sadness in my life. Such pain and anger and pure disappointment in someone. Eventually, I found the strength to sit up, leaves clinging to my hair and pine needles to my sweater— but I didn't care about any of that.

I felt empty.

Why had this happened? After all this time?

How could it *possibly* have happened? How did I never see it coming?

I never in a million years thought I would fall in love with Ryan Rupert, of all people. And when I did finally come to trust him, I believed he would never break my heart. I felt like I could open up to him, tell him anything, and, no matter what, he would never judge me. He would always keep me safe.

I had *believed* that!

I remembered the time he'd tried to save my fall when I fell out of the canoe—even though he'd pretended he hadn't.

I remembered the night he ruffled my hair, and we ate pizza, and he comforted me in the bathroom during a thunderstorm. And then I'd kissed him for the first time and realized how much I liked him.

I remembered him saving me from a jellyfish sting, and protecting me from Courtney on the island.

And there were countless other memories, too—sweet dates he'd taken me on, silly moments we'd had at each other's houses, intimate moments we'd shared so often.....

Now, it was over. Like it had never even happened. What the *hell* was I supposed to do now?

I considered going back to the cabin, but that was the last thing I wanted. I couldn't face Ryan again right now. Perhaps not ever. But I couldn't stay here in these woods forever, either.

Somehow, I managed to gather the strength to get to my feet. I began to aimlessly walk, unsure where I was going. I just had to do *something*—I felt like I couldn't escape all the thoughts in my brain.

Before I knew it, I'd come across the hiking path that we'd walked a few days earlier, and decided to walk back to the top from here.

I wasn't the kind of girl to do things like this alone, but I didn't know what else to do. I was alone now, whether I liked it or not.

Despite knowing that, there was a part of me that hoped Ryan would come to his senses and ask for me back. After all, I *wanted* to be with him. That would-n't change, at least, not for some time.

But *I* was the one who was powerless. This was *his* decision, not mine—and it couldn't be me who asked for him.

Eventually, I reached the top and spotted someone already up here, sitting behind the railing at the lookout's edge where a light, clear morning sky now greeted us.

Disappointment crashed through me—I'd wanted to be alone—until I recognized the familiar head of black hair.

"Melissa?"

She swivelled around to face me, and she looked as bad as I felt.

"Oh...hey, Aubany," she said, her tone dull and her eyes puffy from crying. She noted my own eyes and added, "Oh, shit—it's morning already, isn't it? I'm so sorry if I made you guys worry—I couldn't be there any longer knowing it was Lewis' cabin...."

I walked up to her. Melissa was my best friend since childhood. If there was anyone I wanted to talk to right now, it was her—and though I didn't wish a breakup upon anyone, it was even better that she knew *exactly* what I was going through right now.

I broke down into sobs next to her immediately, and she startled. I felt her arm wrap around my shoulders.

"Aubany, I'm sorry—"

"No, Ryan broke up with me," I choked out. I felt her arm stiffen.

"What?" she asked, looking stunned. "*Why?* The guy is clearly crazy about you!"

That made me sob even harder. She wrapped her arms tightly around me and the familiar scent of her pomegranate shampoo wafted past me. I didn't mind her seeing me ugly cry, snot running from my nose and all. She'd seen worse throughout the years.

"What happened?" she asked quietly.

So I told her—about Ryan's intentions to be a singer, about how he believed we couldn't be together...and as I was talking, I realized the absolute worst part.

"He loves me just as much," I breathed quietly. "So much that he's trying to do the right thing by me—but that means he's hurting as much as I am, and I can't do anything to comfort him."

My voice wavered on those last few words and I crumbled again. Melissa sat by, listening to my every word.

"I'm sorry, Aubany," Melissa said finally. "You don't deserve this...and Ryan, well, you know how I feel about him, but he *does* love you. As much as I hate to say it, I'm glad he's doing this—because it's the right thing for him to do."

I sniffled. I knew she was right, but her words didn't make me feel any better.

"I wish it wasn't like this," I whispered. "I wish there was another way."

"Unfortunately for the two of us, we appear to have bad luck when it comes to men," Melissa replied, that dull tone returning to her voice. "I'm just glad I have my best friend right now."

"I'm glad I have you, too," I replied, squeezing her hand. "I'm sorry about Lewis."

"It's okay," she replied evenly, but she didn't say anything more.

And so, the two of us sat there looking out over the rolling mountains and lake. Looking at the lake reminded me of ice skating with Ryan, of that strange song that was playing, and I couldn't help feeling that *this* was where love came to die.

CHAPTER FIFTEEN

DISCOVERING A DEVIL

Ryan's POV

The bustle in the café was a low murmur in my ears.

Savannah and Alex sat across from me at a rounded table, each one taking turns to eye me worriedly. I tried my best to ignore them, turning my gaze to the wooden floor instead.

"Are you sure we should be out here?" Alex asked finally. I looked up to see him scanning the busy café, which was filled with tables and chairs and local customers.

Savannah brushed him off.

"Please—Courtney wouldn't dare attack us in a busy place like this," she replied, but I noticed the way her eyes also flickered warily. She fidgeted with her hands and added, "Besides, we needed to. Being holed up in that cabin after last night, and this morning...."

She trailed off, biting her lip, then looked away from me.

Alex sighed, then met my gaze.

"Have you heard from her?" he asked me. I barely shook my head in response, and any words I had died in my throat.

What have I done?

Once again, my thoughts went round in my heart like a tornado. Had I just made the biggest mistake of my life? Had I just ruined everything? Or was she better off now?

How can she be better off with Courtney around?

I gritted my teeth and shifted in my chair. Thankfully, the waitress arrived in that moment to bring us our orders.

"A caramel latte," she said, placing the cup down in front of me.

I stared down at the swirls in the mug, and a heaviness came over my chest. The smell reminded me of how Aubany made me coffee on Nula Island. The smell *alone* was enough to drive me insane.

Once the waitress was gone, I slowly pushed the cup away from me.

Savannah pulled her phone out of her bag and began pressing numbers on the screen.

"I'll check on our cars again," she said, before standing and crossing the room with her phone to her ear.

The sooner we got out of here, the better. Aubany would be safer with her family. And then we wouldn't have to face each other. Knowing I would have to see her again before all this was over...

"We can't just sit around here all day," Alex said, bringing me back to Earth. He ran a hand through his curly hair, as if thinking. "We could go to my grandmother's house. I'm sure she wouldn't mind."

"Yeah, okay," I replied, my tone empty.

He studied me for a moment, before adding,

"You know, it's not too late. You can still talk about what happened with her—"

"I can't," I said quickly. "It...took so much strength to say it the first time. If I went back on my word--or worse, if I had to do it to her again..."

I felt a lump in my throat, and Alex nodded, dropping it.

I blinked quickly to evade the tears threatening to form and swallowed hard. No, this was for the best. I just had to accept that and get through it.

Savannah came back, her boots clacking and bracelets jingling as she sat once more.

"So, the good news is, the Ute is ready to go. But my car won't be ready until tomorrow."

She met my gaze and added,

"If you wanted, I could drive Aubany and Melissa back tomorrow. I know you don't like Lewis, but if it was easier, you could go back with him today."

It was a smart plan. And yet, the idea of leaving Aubany here all alone...

"I'll think about it," I replied. She nodded carefully, then shifted as an uncomfortable look crossed her face.

"And...Aubany just texted me. She's asking where we are."

She paused, clearly waiting for my response to guide her. I repressed a sigh and swallowed hard again.

"Tell her to come here," I managed. "I don't want her out there alone."

"Right. Okay," Savannah said, and her fingers began flying over her phone screen once more.

I leaned back in my chair and tried not to think about being in the same room as her. My eyes fixed on a lightbulb above us, and I stared until my eyes began to water from the glare.

"Where's Melissa?" Alex asked, breaking the silence. "Is she with Aubany? I haven't seen or heard from her since last night."

"I don't know—I'll ask," Savannah said as she typed.

We waited in mostly silence, as Alex and Savannah sipped their coffees. The two of them attempted small talk with me, making comments here and there about the café, but I tuned them out. Eventually, the bell above the door tinkled and I could tell from the way Savannah straightened up that Aubany had arrived.

I couldn't bring myself to turn around.

"Hey," I heard her say from behind us. She moved straight past me, pulling up a chair a short distance away and angling it so her back was to me.

I tried not to notice the hurt that shot through my chest watching her.

"Thanks for letting me meet with you. Melissa's gone to talk to Lewis back at the cabin."

"She has?" Savannah asked, raising an eyebrow. "I didn't think they had anything left to scream at each other after last night."

"Well, apparently he still has things to say," Aubany muttered. "How long have you guys been here?"

"A while," Savannah replied, stirring her coffee with her spoon. "We thought it was better to get out of the cabin—and Alex was saying we could spend the day at his grandmother's house."

Aubany seemed to brighten at that suggestion.

"Really?" she asked. "Yeah—that sounds great! Are you guys nearly done? Can we go now?"

She was practically jumping out of her seat.

"Sure," Savannah said, collecting her purse. She then noticed my untouched coffee. "Oh, Ryan—you haven't finished yet."

"Haven't started, rather," Alex pointed out.

"I'm not thirsty, after all," I replied quickly, getting to my feet. "Come on, let's go."

I turned to leave before I had a chance to catch Aubany's expression. It would undoubtedly send regret through every inch of my body all over again.

~

When we reached Alex's grandmother's house, I took in the country cottage exterior and nicely trimmed bushes in the front garden. The door opened and a frail, old woman with tufts of white hair and a simple, beige dress greeted us.

"Oh, Alex, dear—you're back so soon!" she exclaimed, shuffling forward to wrap her arms around him. She then noticed us and added,

"Oh, and I see you've bought friends. How lovely!" She waved us all inside. "Come in, come in. I'll find something to eat."

"Oh, no—that's okay Mrs. Newman," Savannah breezed. "We just came from breakfast."

My stomach grumbled in protest, but I didn't complain. The four of us ventured into the house, where an overbearing vanilla scent greeted us. Plush, cream carpet and an electric heater were the first things I noticed upon stepping into the cosy living room. There were many antiques on the shelves and a very simple lounge.

"Well, how about some water? I'll fetch a pitcher," Mrs. Newman insisted, squeezing her grandson's shoulder as Savannah beamed at her. Aubany wandered away from us, putting distance between us as she busied herself looking through the bookshelves at the many photographs and vases.

I turned away to focus on the other side of the room, which was mostly bare.

Alex crossed the room to sit on the lounge, and pulled open a drawer in the coffee table, revealing a stack of playing cards.

"Should we do something? Otherwise, I could turn on TV?"

The idea of us all sitting around, playing cards and having to speak to each other didn't appeal one bit.

"Actually, I need some air. Why don't you guys decide?"

I turned to head back out the front. At least this way Aubany could take her mind off of things without having to endure my presence. I slipped out the front into the brisk air once more and sat down on the front steps.

After a moment, I buried my head in my hands, and finally the tears came.

They didn't stop for a long time.

~

Hours later, when my eyes looked less red and puffy, I went back inside to check on the group. As I walked down the hallway towards the living room, I spotted Mrs. Newman and the others gathered around on the lounge from the doorway. They were flipping through an old photo album.

I hovered in the doorway so as not to disturb them.

"Oh, and this was my wedding day," she said, pointing to one of the pages. "Yes, I remember it like it was yesterday."

"Your dress was beautiful," Savannah gushed, looking at the picture. "Do you still have it?"

"Actually, I do," Mrs. Newman replied in a crinkly voice, her expression delighted. "Would you like to see it?"

Savannah's eyes lit up. "I would *love* to see it!"

"Well, you wait right here and I'll bring it out," Mrs. Newman said, patting her hand before getting up slowly from the couch. She shuffled out of the room.

It was then that Savannah noticed me hovering and she smiled.

"Feeling better?" she asked. Aubany looked up and our gazes met. She instantly looked back down and busied herself by flipping a page in the photo album.

"Yeah," I said, walking over to them. Alex and Savannah were looking at me, but Aubany let out a small noise in her throat and leaned closer to the photo album page.

"Oh...my God," she breathed. Frowning, the three of us huddled closer to see what she was looking at. In the pages of the album was a newspaper clipping, and in the photo were two familiar faces, both roughly nine or ten years old.

I stared at the young boy and my gut twisted.

"Is...that Lewis?" I asked, frowning.

"And Courtney?" Savannah added, her voice quivering. The two were standing together in front of an older woman. It was staged like a family portrait.

"What does the article say?" I pressed, feeling the urge to rip it from Aubany's hands and devour every word.

"It's hard to read—it's so old," she said, squinting. "Eight-year-old girl detained after stalking scandal...."

Her eyes scanned quickly, then widened.

"Last Tuesday afternoon, eight-year-old Courtney Madsen was arrested by police. They had reason to believe she suffered from an obsessive disorder of extreme levels, and discovered she had spent months collecting pictures and stolen possessions of males resembling a similar physical appearance."

"What the hell?" Savannah breathed. "But why is Lewis in the photo? Is it him?"

"It doesn't say. Just that Courtney was supposed to undergo a psychic evaluation—"

She paused, her eyes darting quickly as she scanned.

"No, wait...here!" she tapped the article excitedly. "Police were informed about the ordeal by the detainee's half-brother, Lewis Kellington, who claimed he *only wanted to help her.*"

My blood ran cold.

"*Brother?*" I repeated. "Lewis is Courtney's brother?"

"Half-brother," Alex corrected, as he read. Savannah rounded on him, ripping the album from Aubany's hands and waving it in his face.

"Alex—why does your grandmother have this?" she cried, panic plastered all over her face. "And how did you not know?"

He recoiled, batting the album away.

"I don't know—I only visit my grandma once every couple of years. And I don't go through her stuff! I guess she kept this because it was local news or something...."

"In the same album as her wedding photos?" I pressed, folding my arms. He shrugged flippantly as Aubany reached out to snatch it back from Savannah.

"Maybe it's the only folder she has with plastic sleeves," Aubany said, flicking one of the pages as she continued to read.

"Exactly," Alex pointed out, crossing his arms. "The clipping's old. Look, I don't know, okay?"

"The family has requested privacy during this up-setting ordeal..." Aubany murmured, as she finished scanning the article. "This article must be at least nine years old or something."

She looked up and met my gaze with fear in her eyes.

"Do you think Lewis is the reason Courtney is here? Do you think it's how she found us?"

I ran a hand through my hair, considering the idea.

"Possibly…I don't know, Aubs—"

We both cringed as the nickname slipped out. I guess I'd have to break that habit. I did my best to smooth it over.

"We don't even know the nature of their relationship. Didn't Melissa say he wasn't close with his sister or something?"

Aubany's eyes widened, jolting as if an electric shock just went through her.

"Oh, my God," she cried, leaping from the couch. "*Melissa!*"

"What?"

Aubany rushed past me towards the front door, gesturing for me to follow.

"Ryan—Melissa and Lewis are alone at the cabin. *Alone!* And Courtney's out there! And if they're working together—what if he hurts her?"

Realization swept through me like a coursing flood.

Of course.

This was almost too easy. First, they'd get to Aubany's best friend. *Then her.*

"We have to get back to the cabin," I said firmly. *"Now!"*

CHAPTER SIXTEEN

SECRETS REVEALED

Aubany's POV

My heart beat wildly as we ran back to the cabin. There was no time to detour and get Savannah's car. My lungs ached, but fear had seized every inch of my body—fear for what might have become of my friend. I couldn't stop running no matter how hard it became to breathe.

Despite everything, I felt safer with Ryan at my side. He kept pace with me, his eyes as wide with panic as mine.

We were nearly there when Savannah collapsed heavily on the dirt driveway.

"I can't keep going," she rasped, a hand grasping her chest. "I can't breathe."

I felt as puffed as she looked. My lungs felt like they were on fire at this point, and I could barely find the breath to return any words.

"Stay here," Ryan breathed. "We'll keep going."

"I'll catch up," she promised, and Alex said he'd stay with her.

That meant it was just Ryan and I.

Up against Lewis...and possibly Courtney, too.

I couldn't bring myself to run again, so we settled for a brisk walk. I kept swallowing, trying to fill my lungs with air and wet my parched throat. But the thought of facing Courtney paired with the marathon I'd just run caused it to dry up again.

"What if Melissa's dead?" I whispered, remembering the last time I'd seen Courtney. The way she'd snapped and plunged that knife into my gut without a second thought. What if we walked in and there was only blood?

Ryan's hand entwined with mine, startling me. He gripped it, strong and firm, and returned a grave expression. My stomach twisted.

I realized he wasn't going to tell me everything would be fine...because that might not be true at all.

I wanted to rip my hand out of his, but I couldn't bring myself to. The sense of familiarity and safety it created was almost like a drug.

We finally reached the end of the driveway, and the two of us stared at the cabin. It had seemed so beautiful when we first arrived. Now, it was like a haunted house—the last place I ever wanted to step foot in again.

Despite feeling that way, I thought of Melissa again and impulsively rushed forward. It was like my head was telling me one thing but my body was doing the opposite. Everything inside me screamed to turn around, but my hand reached for the doorknob and turned it. I pushed hard on the wood, bursting into the cabin.

Nothing but a creaky echo and dim emptiness greeted us. All the furniture was where we had left it. There was no one here.

"Melissa!" I screamed, stepping into the house. I felt Ryan's presence behind me. My voice ricocheted off every beam and hollow. "Melissa, are you in here?"

A thud from upstairs made my head whip around, and she emerged from one of the bedrooms, resting her hands on the mezzanine railing.

"Aubany?" she replied, with a frown. "Why are you screaming like that?"

"Oh, my God," I sobbed, fresh tears springing into my eyes as relief shuddered through me. I raced up the stairs and straight into her arms, clutching her tightly.

"You're okay," I whispered over and over, and I felt her tense.

"What the *hell* is up with you?" she asked, shifting out of my grasp and stepping back to take me in. "Why wouldn't I be okay?"

"Where's Lewis?" I asked frantically, scanning the cabin. "Melissa, we have to leave. Right now—"

"She's not going anywhere," a voice replied from behind me. I spun sharply, finding myself face to face with Lewis.

I felt the blood drain from my face. Ryan made a sound from downstairs.

"Get back!" I cried, stumbling into Melissa. She yelped.

"Aubany—" she tried to protest, but I grabbed her arm and pulled her back with me. Ryan was thundering up the stairs, and Lewis threw his hands up in protest.

"Woah, what's—"

"Don't lay a hand on her," Ryan growled, pushing past Lewis. "On *either* of them."

Lewis' gaze darkened.

"Why should I listen to you about what I can and can't do with my *girlfriend*, Rupert?"

"Don't you mean *ex*-girlfriend?" I seethed pointedly, as Ryan came to stand with us.

"Aubany, stop it!" Melissa protested, shifting past me towards Lewis now. The two of them stood opposite us on the landing now. "Lewis and I have been talking—"

"Lewis is *dangerous!*" I cut in, trying to grab her again, but she leapt back from me. My gaze turned pleading. "Melissa! Lewis is Courtney's *half-brother!*"

I expected shock, but there was none. Instead, her expression was...*sympathetic?*

"I know, Aubany," she replied gently. "He told me."

Like an eruption, anger bubbled within me and my eyes boggled out of my head.

"*What?*"

How long had she known?

She exchanged a quick glance with him and added,

"Aubany, listen to me—"

I leapt back from her, betrayal washing over me as my jaw dropped.

"No don't—just don't!"

I began to shake. Was there *anybody* here I could trust? My eyes burned with hot tears.

"You're meant to be my best friend! You *know* what Courtney did to me!"

"I said listen to me!" Melissa pleaded, her green eyes wide as she stepped forward. I'd rarely seen Melissa beg, but I was too upset to care.

"Where is she?" I demanded, shifting my gaze to Lewis. All the hairs were rising on the back of my neck.

"Who?" he asked calmly.

"*Courtney.*"

"She's not here, if that's what you're asking."

There was a pause between us all for a moment. Then I clenched my fists.

"I want to see inside the locked bedroom."

Ryan shifted beside me.

"Aubany, we already checked—"

"*I need to see it!*"

My outburst made everyone jump. I hadn't realized my hands were shaking until my clenched fists began to ache. I felt like I was slowly losing my grasp on reality.

Ryan was leaving me.

Melissa had sided with Lewis.

Savannah had stayed behind.

I was alone here. I was all on my own, and I hadn't been truly alone in such a long time it scared me. I didn't *want* to do this on my own. Courtney was after me—and without Ryan…without my friends…I felt like a sitting duck.

"Okay," Lewis relented, slowly reaching for his pocket. "I'm going to unlock the door with my key. It's in my pocket."

My gaze was locked on him as he pulled a silver key from his pocket, like he said. I let him walk past me, crossing to the end of the landing to face the locked room.

I heard the *clink* as the key slid into the lock.

I held my breath.

For all I knew, Courtney really was in there.

She could be holding a knife.

Or a gun.

The door swung open and I braced myself to be shot...but the room was empty.

Lewis turned to me and waved for me to go in.

"Search it, if you like. There's nobody in there."

I hesitated, terrified she might be hiding behind the door. But I somehow found the strength to take a step forward. Every muscle in my body felt like lead as I inched towards the room, and slowly peered my head inside.

Empty. Just as Lewis had said.

Turning to him, I narrowed my gaze.

"You led her here, didn't you?"

He raised an eyebrow at me.

"You're referring to Courtney again?"

I nodded, and he sighed.

"It's complicated, Aubany. Why don't you let me explain—"

"You *lied* to us, Lewis!" I snapped. "You put us all in danger! Were you reporting to Courtney the whole time since we got back from Nula Island? Is that all Melissa is to you? A way to get closer to me?"

"You've got it all wrong," he insisted firmly. I let out a dry laugh.

"I don't need to hear any more from you, Lewis," I shot back. "Why would I trust you when you're her *half-brother?*"

He glared back at me. "There's something you need to know—"

"Aubany!" came a call from downstairs. I recognized it as Savannah's voice, and Lewis immediately shut his mouth.

Relief flooded through me at the prospect of more backup.

"Ryan—let's get our things. We can't stay here," I said, turning my back on Lewis.

"Aubany, wait," Melissa said, following me as I stormed into the bedroom Ryan and I had been staying in. "You can't leave yet."

"Get out!" I shouted at her over my shoulder. "I don't want to see you right now!"

"I can't," she insisted, this time in a lower voice. She glanced towards the landing, where the others were still crowded. "It's not safe for you yet. For any of us."

"Okay, you know what?" I snapped, folding my arms. "I'm tired of this! I don't want to play games, or solve riddles. Either be straight with me or get *out,* because I'm *so* not talking to you right now."

I waited, giving her a moment to speak, but she looked torn. Her eyes darted back to the landing, and to me.

"Lewis isn't the bad guy here," she said, her voice so quiet I could barely hear it. "We need to stick together."

"Stick to Lewis then, if you care about him so much," I shot back darkly. "I'm going home."

I pulled the drawers open and began chucking my clothes into my suitcase. After a moment, Ryan walked into the room and started retrieving his own stuff. When we had finished, we wordlessly walked past them both to join Savannah and Alex at the foot of the stairs. I realized they'd packed their bags too.

"Our cars will be ready to go tomorrow," Savannah reminded me. "We can stay at Alex's grandmother's tonight and leave first thing in the morning."

She looked over at Melissa and added,

"You're welcome too, if you change your mind. But not *him.*"

Her gaze landed on Lewis with a glare. He frowned back.

With that, the four of us turned and walked out of the cabin.

CHAPTER SEVENTEEN

LOVE AS DEEP AS A FOREST

Aubany's POV

When we returned, Alex's grandmother seemed confused as to why we'd left so suddenly.

"I came out with my wedding dress, but you were all gone," she said, shaking her head. "You young ones sure do get around."

"Can we stay here tonight?" Savannah asked, as we all grouped in the living room once more.

She eyed the four of us with an uncertain expression.

"Well, I suppose we could make it work. Except I only have one guest room, and a single bed."

Savannah shook her head. "I don't mind sleeping on the floor. One of the others can have the couch, like I did last time."

She frowned.

"Well, as long as you don't mind, I'm happy for you to stay here tonight. I'll see if I can find some more blankets, at least."

She shuffled off again towards the stairs, and Savannah let out a relieved breath.

"I can't *believe* it's true," she muttered. "Lewis is really Courtney's half-brother."

"And Melissa doesn't care," I added bitterly, folding my arms. Ryan glanced at me, looking as if he wanted to comfort me, but he didn't. That hurt even more.

Dinner that night was a fast and quiet affair. Nobody was in much of a talking mood, and Mrs. Newman's casserole was a little too soggy for my liking.

After that, she headed up to bed, and Alex took the upstairs bedroom while the rest of us made do with the blankets we had downstairs. Ryan and I made makeshift beds in the small space—barely far enough away from each other.

He looked at me again as we were climbing into bed, like he wanted to say something, but again didn't. I bit back the urge to snap at him to spit it out. Instead, I climbed into my own bed and rolled onto my back.

Savannah flicked the light off.

"Goodnight, you two," she said, crossing the room towards her bed on the couch. "Are you sure you want to sleep down there?"

"Yes," Ryan and I both said in unison. A strange silence filled the air, and I heard Savannah's sheets rustling in the dark as she got comfortable.

Then there was silence. Minutes and minutes of it. I felt like I was lying there for hours in the darkness. It was at *least* forty minutes before I heard Savannah's soft snores.

I grimaced. I couldn't sleep, knowing Ryan was mere inches away from me. Knowing I could easily reach for his hand and grasp it.

As if reading my thoughts, I heard his quiet voice break through the silence.

"Aubany."

Hope and disdain washed through me all at once. I startled slightly as his fingers crept into mine, and an ache formed in my heart.

"I really am sorry."

A lump formed in my throat. There were so many things I wanted to say in return...and so many things I could think to do. But with Savannah sleeping on the couch next to us, it hardly felt private.

"Ryan," I managed to croak out. "I can't do this right now."

"Well, I can't *not* do this right now," he replied quietly. "I can't sleep by your side without saying anything. I can't act as if there was never anything between us knowing there was...and I ruined it all."

Tears were streaming down my cheeks in the dark.

"You must hate me right now," he murmured.

"Hate you?" I echoed, suppressing a dry laugh. "How could I hate you? Even though you've broken my heart into thousands of pieces, I don't think I could ever hate you."

I rolled over to face him properly, studying the outline of his handsome face in the dark. My heart broke as the next words came out choked,

"I will always *love* you."

It sounded stupid. The idea that I could love someone forever. That five years from now, when we haven't spoken a word to one another, I could still remember all his quirks and mannerisms and feel the same amount of love that I did right now.

But I couldn't imagine loving him any less than I already did. It didn't feel possible that my feelings for him would ever fade away.

I heard him sniffle, and he squeezed my hand a little.

"I'll always love you too."

I bit back a sob and squeezed my eyes shut. I felt his hand stroking my hair as he pulled me close to him and held me, and, just like that, I melted. All at once everything was okay, and yet worse at the same time. I knew eventually he would let go and that would be that. This would be the last time I was ever in his arms. My last chance to hold him back and show him just how much he meant to me.

"I'm sorry, Aubs," he whispered in my hair, as the soothing strokes continued.

I was sobbing quietly into his chest now.

"Why did you do this to me?" I whispered back, clutching him tightly. "Why did you let me fall in love with you?"

"I'm sorry," he said again, as my sobs shook my body.

"This was easier when I hated you."

"I know."

"You should never have let me trust you."

"I know."

"You should never have helped me overcome my fears on Nula Island—"

A pause, and the sobs ceased as I looked up at him in the dark.

"Don't say that," he said, cupping my cheek. "You're a better person because of it."

"Because of *you,*" I whispered back.

"No, that was all you, Aubs."

Surprise washed over me as I considered his words. He stared back at me with such a genuine gaze.

"You're stronger than you think."

He paused, taking a shaky breath, before adding,

"That's how I know you'll be fine without me."

The warmth in my heart thawed over instantly.

"I don't feel that way," I mumbled, as tears formed again.

"You don't have to. But know that I can see things in you that you don't see for yourself."

There was silence after that for a while, and we stayed in each other's arms. I nuzzled into his chest and tried not to think about the reality waiting for us when morning came.

"I wish I wasn't hurting you," he whispered finally. "But you know I'm doing this for you, right?"

"I know," I murmured back, as sleep and exhaustion from the events of the day began to overtake me.

"And if I could go back and prevent you from falling for me...even though I'd be giving up the best seven months of my life...I would."

"I know."

Another pause, and my mind seemed miles away as I heard his final words.

"Even though I was already in love with you."

If I said *I know* back, I didn't remember it.

CHAPTER EIGHTEEN

DEAL WITH THE DEVIL

Ryan's POV

I waited until Aubany's breathing became slow and steady before shifting gently out of her grasp. Pulling the blanket over her, I stood in the crisp night air and collected my phone from where I'd left it on the coffee table.

If she knew I was doing this, she would lose her shit.

I crept through the house and carefully unlocked the back door, slipping out into the even colder air. Despite my thick hoodie and long tracksuit pants, I felt goose bumps creep up my arms.

I held up my phone and flicked the screen on to re-read the text message I'd received earlier.

Meet me outside Alex's grandmother's house to-night.

I headed around the side of the house, past various bushes and flower beds, then slipped through a creaky gate. Two lines of gravel marked where a car clearly drove in and out to park on the side of the house. I followed that path until I spotted him waiting near the curb.

Lewis spotted me and straightened up, walking towards me.

"We don't have much time," he said when he reached me. "I need your help—but first, I want to explain some things to you."

Lewis was far from my favourite person, but I couldn't help but feel like I should at least listen to his side of the story. Aubany had jumped to conclusions, and I'd wanted to support her in the moment. But I wish she'd let Lewis talk earlier.

"Fine," I relented. "But hurry up. I'm freezing out here."

"I know that this looks bad," Lewis began slowly. "Me being Courtney's half-brother. It's true—we grew up together. But we lost touch for a long time. It wasn't until recently that she found me again."

I indicated with a nod for him to continue. He ran a despairing hand through his hair and began to pace.

"That story I told? On our first day here? It was about us—how we got separated. Our mother...."

He paused for a moment, as if deep in thought.

"I *thought* she was dead. But as it turns out...she might not be."

He crossed the yard to sit on a large rock that was part of one of the flowerbeds, clasping his hands together loosely and leaning his elbows on his knees.

"What's your point, Lewis?" I asked, following him across the yard.

He met my gaze.

"The point is that when Courtney reached out to me again, it was after you guys returned from Nula Island. She bargained with me—asked me to get you guys here and to help her...in exchange for information about our mother's whereabouts."

I folded my arms.

"So, what was the plan? You get us here, you take us out one by one until Aubany and I are the only ones left? Was it you who tampered with her bike? With our cars?"

"No," he said quickly. "The bike—that wasn't me. The cars...maybe I did that part. It's complicated—"

"I get it, you're in cahoots—"

"Stop interrupting!" he snapped back, and I recoiled slightly. He let out a single breath, burying his head in his hands.

"Look," he ground out. "I can't reveal the most critical parts without risking my chance to find my mother again. I've asked and searched, but nobody knows where she is. If there's even a *slight* chance that Courtney knows what happened to her...I need that information."

Annoyance shot through me.

"So, you'd endanger us to find your own mother?"

"At first...I did," he admitted. "This was months ago—before I knew either of you well. Melissa and I had been dating, but it wasn't until you and Aubany got together that we started talking more at school. Otherwise, it was just Melissa and her, or Melissa and I. So I didn't realize that"—He paused for a moment, looking pained--"that I would regret it. Aubany is Melissa's best friend, and she doesn't deserve any of this."

"So why did you bring us here after all realizing that?"

He shook his head.

"I didn't have a choice. Again—I can't tell you everything going on, but you're not truly safe until you get out of this town. Except you can't tell anyone I'm telling you this. Or that you know any of this. I just needed you to know how I'm involved and why."

I sighed. I felt more confused than I did before. Part of his story was vague, and I needed a clearer answer.

"Lewis, what do you want from us?"

"I have a plan," he said slowly. "One that will keep Aubany safe, and I can still get the information I need. But I need to deliver on my end of the deal in order for her to tell me what she knows."

I indicated for him to continue.

"Tomorrow, Aubany needs to leave with Savannah and Alex. But you need to stay here. All I need is for you to have a single meeting with Courtney—"

I stepped back.

"No way," I replied firmly. "I'm *not* doing that again."

"There's more, though," he insisted, almost pleadingly. I paused, waiting, and he continued.

"I have a plan so that the two of you can have your meeting—but I'll tip off the cops to the location and let them know you're keeping her occupied. They'll find her, catch her, and take her back to the institute to get the treatment she needs. I'll have what I need, and you'll be safe and free to go home."

I hesitated, but there was one glimmering opportunity in this plan.

No more Courtney.

For *good*—no more worrying where she was, whether she'd show up again. Aubany would be safe forever. Even if I left for LA...she'd be safe.

The cops hadn't been able to catch her, but she'd reveal herself for me because she wanted to be with me. That sparked a new question.

"Lewis, what's...*wrong* with your sister?" I asked, and winced at my lack of tact. He shook his head again.

"I wish I knew," he replied. "This all started when we were young. She saw a boy with black hair and blue eyes on the hiking trail behind our house one day."

My eyes widened. That memory...of that day. The girl...

Lewis' eyes widened suddenly.

"Oh, the cabin—that's not our holiday home. It's our family home," he added quickly. Somehow, knowing that—and knowing we'd *stayed* there—sent even more chills up my spine.

"Anyway, she became *obsessed* with finding him. She could only ever substitute in her stalking, but it was never the exact guy she spotted that day. I think it drove her crazy that she couldn't find him again. I'm not sure what's off in her brain to make her think that way, but it's who she is."

He paused, thinking again.

"At the end of the day, she's still my sister. I don't want anything bad to happen to her. I want her in the right care, with people who can help her. But she'll never listen to me if I ask her to go back to the institute on her own. This is the only way."

"Lewis," I said slowly. "It was me on that hiking trail."

I gauged his reaction, but he didn't seem surprised.

"Does she know it was me?"

He nodded.

"How does she know that?"

He avoided my gaze.

"That's part of the thing I can't tell you," he admitted. "But yes, she knows it was you. And she remembers Aubany, too. I think it's another thing triggering her hate towards her. This whole time, Aubany has been by your side, while Courtney was searching and could never find you."

"Do you think she'd kill Aubany?" I asked, the question making my throat dry up.

"Honestly?"

His expression was grim.

"I wouldn't put it past her. If she was standing in the way of you, I think she'd do anything to get as close to you as possible. I don't think she understands the consequences of her actions...or realizes exactly what she'd be doing if she ever did hurt Aubany. But I don't think she's capable of feeling remorse for her."

A resolve settled in me in that moment. I couldn't let that happen.

"Then I'll help you," I said quietly. "But I'm doing it for Aubany—not you."

"I had a feeling you would," Lewis replied, getting to his feet. "In that case, here's what we need to do."

CHAPTER NINETEEN

PARTING WAYS

Aubany's POV

The next morning, Ryan and I sat on opposite sides of Mrs. Newman's breakfast table. We both had mugs of coffee, but neither of us were drinking. Ryan refused to look at me.

It was as if last night had never happened.

Savannah and Alex had gone to get Savannah's car from the shop. They would be back any second, and then we would be leaving.

"I hope you have a safe trip back," Mrs. Newman said, as she shuffled around the kitchen. "Are you sure you don't want something to eat before you go? I have some nice porridge I can make."

"No, thanks," I said quickly, forcing a smile. "Thanks for letting us stay here last night."

"Yeah—thank you," Ryan added earnestly, and he finally took a sip of his coffee.

The sound of gravel crunched through the open window, followed by an engine, and Mrs. Newman peered out.

"Ah—they're back," she informed us. "I'll help you with your bags."

"Oh, no," I said quickly, getting to my feet. "Please, it's okay, Mrs. Newman. You've done enough."

Ryan and I went to fetch our things and carried them to the front door, which opened just as we reached it. Savannah and Alex stepped inside. They moved past us to say goodbye to Mrs. Newman and get their own bags.

Ryan and I headed down the small front steps towards the boot of the car. I hoisted my bag in, and Ryan dropped his bags to help me.

"I'm fine," I protested, but he helped anyway. As soon as my bags were in, I reached to help him with his, but he placed a hand over mine to stop me.

"I'm not coming with you," he said suddenly. I froze, frowning at him.

"What do you mean?" I asked slowly.

"Savannah and Alex are going to take you back with them. But I'm staying here," he revealed. "There's something I need to finish with Lewis."

"What are you talking about?" I demanded, my nostrils flaring. "You can't stay here, Ryan! It's not safe!"

"I've already made up my mind," he replied firmly, folding his arms. "And besides—we're not together anymore."

"That doesn't mean you can just—"

I stopped myself, realizing that I had no control over him. Not even when we were dating did I have control over him. He simply *chose* to listen to me and respect my requests.

Now none of that even mattered. He wasn't obligated to listen to me at all.

My mouth opened, then closed. I couldn't find any words to make him stay. Instead, hot tears formed in my eyes against my will.

"Please don't do this," I begged finally.

His expression gave away nothing. Where was the person who had consoled me last night? What had happened to his kind words? Had I dreamed it?

Now he was like a statue. Like any trace of romantic feelings towards me had vanished.

I turned away from him, unable to face it anymore, as Savannah and Alex stepped out of the house and came to join us.

"Will you be okay?" Savannah asked Ryan, and he nodded.

So she had known.

It felt like every day, another secret was being kept from me. Another person turning against me behind my back.

"Ring me when you're done to let me know you're okay?" Savannah asked, and Ryan nodded again. I refused to speak to all of them, folding my arms in silent protest.

Savannah turned to me.

"Okay. We're ready to go," she said. Wordlessly, I opened the back door and climbed in. I made a point to slam it shut, and I noticed Alex and Savannah exchange a glance. Their goodbyes to Ryan were murmured from outside, and then they also got in the car. Savannah ignited the engine and backed out of the driveway.

I risked a glance out the window. Mrs. Newman was standing in the doorway waving, and Ryan was watching the car.

Watching me.

I glared back at him, my eyes burning at him, before turning away once more.

It wasn't until we'd driven away when the tears finally began rolling down my face and I fell defeatedly against the car door.

~

When we reached my house, I felt like an eternity had passed. My mom had been waiting for us, and she rushed out of the house to greet me.

"I am so happy to see you," she said, wrapping her arms around me as I stepped out of the car.

"Mom, please," I replied, wedged between the car and her.

She looked at Savannah and Alex, then her expression dropped.

"Honey, where's Ryan?"

My expression crumpled, and she was immediately horrified.

Savannah quickly stepped in before she could assume the worst.

"He's staying behind," she said quickly. My mom shook her head.

"But I told Josh and Renee that he'd be back today."

"He lied," I said bitterly, moving past them to grab my bags from the car. I dragged them out, and they fell with a *thud* to the ground as I headed for the house.

I heard my mom invite Savannah and Alex inside from behind me, but I continued on ahead. I just needed to be alone right now.

Hours later, I emerged from my bedroom. I'd been in there for hours, curled in a ball on my bed. Avoiding the pictures of Ryan and I that sat on my bookshelf. Trying not to think about him at all.

To my surprise, Savannah and Alex were still downstairs, sitting and talking to my mom and dad at the dining table. I overheard a part of their conversation and realized they were explaining what had happened on the trip.

When I reached the doorway, I cleared my throat to make myself known and all four pairs of eyes locked onto me.

"Oh, hi, sweetheart," Mom greeted, standing. "Would you like a drink? Or something to eat? Savannah and Alex are going to stay the night before they head home tomorrow."

"I'm not hungry," I mumbled, folding my arms. I glanced at Savannah, but I was still upset with her. She must have known, because she offered me a sheepish look.

"You let him stay behind," I said to her, stepping into the room. "You should have told me."

"It was none of my business, Aubany," she replied, a sympathetic expression crossing my face.

I clenched my fists.

"Why didn't you talk him out of it?"

"I tried to!" she cried back. "But he wasn't going to budge. I'm sorry—I really am."

"Ryan can make his own choices," Mom said carefully, glancing between us. "What he does is not for either of you to decide. But his parents aren't happy, I'll say that much."

I sucked in a breath, then let it out slowly.

"I'll go find some bedding for Savannah and Alex," I mumbled, and turned to head back upstairs.

It didn't take me long to find the bedding in our linen cupboard, but I didn't make it back downstairs. Instead, I went back to my room with the blankets, sat on my bed, and stayed there. I was so consumed by my own thoughts that I didn't notice my dad standing in the doorway until he knocked.

"Hey," he greeted, as I looked up. "Can I come in?"

I shrugged, and shifted to make room on the bed for him among the blankets. He carefully sat beside me.

"So...we've heard what happened," he said. "But I wanted to hear it from you. About Ryan."

"What's there to tell?" I replied bitterly. "He stayed behind."

"No—why did he break up with you?" Dad asked.

My bottom lip quivered as he said the words out loud, and I bought my knees up to my chest to hug them there.

"Because...he wants to pursue music," I replied quietly. "And he doesn't think he can do that *and* be with me. At least, not in a way that's fair to me."

Dad seemed confused, frowning at my explanation.

"That's very assuming for someone his age," he replied. "He's acting as if his music career is guaranteed. But he hasn't even gotten into college yet."

I agreed with him, but I shook my head.

"It doesn't matter—he's already decided," I muttered. "It's done now."

"At least it sounds like he's trying to do the right thing by you," Dad added. "But you never know—you guys might get back together. He might realize—"

"Dad, stop it," I cut in quickly. "I don't want false hope. He broke my heart into a thousand pieces and that's about all I can process right now."

"Okay, okay," Dad replied, reaching to rub my back soothingly. Tears burned in my eyes again, but I wiped them away.

"Why does it hurt so much?" I asked finally. "When will it stop hurting?"

Dad seemed thoughtful for a moment.

"It's going to hurt for a while because you've lost something," he explained carefully. "When I went through my first breakup, it took two weeks before the pain became a dull ache. It was still there...but it didn't bother me the way it did before."

I glanced at him.

"Who was she?" I asked. He swallowed hard, and then his own eyes went glassy as he looked away from me.

"Oh, it was just…a girl..." he said, almost absently. "It was a long time ago."

"What happened?"

"Well, you know how it is. People grow apart and...one day, she left. I don't really know why."

He shrugged as he spoke.

"But then I met your mother and I'm happy with her. It's just...the first one always hurts the worst. And you never truly get over it. But the pain goes away, eventually. And you move on."

He looked back at me and rubbed my back again.

"Everything will be okay, honey. It'll work out in the end. You'll see."

I knew he was right, but it didn't feel that way.

He stood and told me dinner would be ready in about an hour, and to come down soon before leaving me be. I stayed where I was for a while, thinking over his words.

My whole life had been Ryan. Now he was gone.

Everything I had planned out for the future had stupidly revolved around him. Now my whole future felt out of whack. Everything seemed so mundane. The idea of going back to school, returning to work...none of it mattered anymore.

And the idea of meeting someone else? I could have laughed. There would never be anyone else. Not like Ryan. I didn't want to start again. I didn't want small talk, or to have to re-build trust, or to create new inside jokes....

I just wanted Ryan.

CHAPTER TWENTY

A THIEF IN THE NIGHT

Aubany's POV

My parents made pleasant conversation with Savannah and Alex as we were eating Mom's roast chicken dinner, but I barely noticed. I spent the entire time scraping my food from one side of my plate to the other.

Mom noticed this after a while, but she didn't say anything. She took my plate when we were done despite the mound of food still piled on it.

"When do you go back to school, Aubany?" Savannah asked from across the table. It was the first time she'd spoken to me all night.

"Monday," I replied, which was four days from now. In that moment, I remembered the homework

Mrs. Denners had handed out and dread filled me at the thought of having to do it in my current mental state.

But it was the perfect excuse to escape to my room again.

"I forgot—I have homework to do," I said, getting to my feet. Dad frowned at me.

"Aubany, you have guests—surely that can wait until tomorrow."

I stopped in my tracks, my hand tightening on the chair I'd been pushing in, and sighed.

"Isn't it clear I don't want company right now?" I asked quietly, shutting my eyes to try and escape the situation.

"Savannah and Alex are your friends, honey. We all know you're hurting…but shutting yourself in your room won't make it better."

"Maybe I don't want it to feel better!" I snapped back. "Maybe I want things to go back to how they were before!"

"Aubany," Mom scolded, emerging from the kitchen. Savannah seemed torn, her eyes burning with guilt and sympathy as she watched me. She rose from the table and circled it.

"Aubany, I'm sorry," she pleaded, reaching to hug me. I stepped back but she pushed through, wrapping her arms around me, and I broke down in her arms. She held me tightly, and I could smell the sweet perfume she always wore.

"I know what Ryan meant to you, and I'm sorry," she whispered. "I'm sorry I lied to you. I'm sorry…."

She pulled away and her eyes burned with guilt.

"I'm sorry I told him to break up with you."

My eyes widened with shock, and I opened my mouth to speak, but she stopped me.

"He came to me for advice. He didn't want to...but he was trying to do the right thing by you. This wasn't easy for him, either. I know you know that, but I'm sorry I had any part in it. I hate seeing you like this."

My hands balled into fists, but all the anger turned to disappointment. I couldn't take one more betrayal from my so-called friends. I hurriedly wiped my eyes, then wordlessly, I turned and stormed down the hall, marching upstairs. I was certain they heard me slam my bedroom door, and I was glad for it.

~

I tapped my pen on the desk, staring at my blank homework. It had been half an hour since I stormed off from dinner, but I hadn't been able to focus. I'd tried music. I'd tried putting Netflix on in the background. I'd tried reading each question aloud.

My thoughts kept drifting back to Ryan. What was he doing right now? What was it that he had to settle back in Blakesky? Was he doing something stupid?

I hated that I cared so much--I wasn't supposed to care anymore. And yet, I couldn't help it.

Eventually, I heard the low murmur of voices downstairs, and the familiar sound of lights flicking off. Everyone was going to bed early—I glanced at the clock on the wall, and it was only 7PM. Knowing my parents, they would make Alex sleep downstairs on the couch and give Savannah the spare room. I remembered how furious they'd been when they heard Renee and Josh had allowed Ryan and I to stay in the same hotel room on Nula Island—and that was *before* we'd been dating.

I tried to refocus on my homework questions, but I knew it was futile. *I should just go to bed*, I thought. *I'll feel better tomorrow*.

But a deeper part of me knew I wouldn't. And that part of me couldn't stop stressing over Ryan. I felt restless and I couldn't sit still. If I had my own car, I'd drive back to Blakesky myself—I just *knew* I would.

I knew how to drive. I often borrowed my mom's car to get to my work shifts. But I probably wouldn't get a car of my own until my eighteenth birthday. It was coming up soon…but not soon enough.

Savannah's car, I thought. Instantly, guilt plagued me at the thought of stealing it. But I was angry at her. And Ryan could be in trouble. Plus, my parents' cars were in the garage. They'd hear the door opening. Savannah's, on the other hand, was parked out on the curb and would be more silent.

I can't leave Ryan in Blakesky alone, I thought, and pressed my fingers to my temples, leaning my elbows on my desk as my thoughts raced. Savannah would be furious. She might never forgive me. But right now, I was *so angry* and disappointed in her that it didn't seem like such a loss.

Resolve settled in me. I got to my feet and quickly packed a bag, throwing the first clothes I found into it. Then I went to the door, flicking off my light switch, and the moment my hand gripped the handle, adrenaline shot through me.

Was I really going to do this?

My hand turned the handle and I quietly crept out onto the landing. Moving through the dark, I used my phone to navigate down the stairs.

I need her keys, I thought, and crept past the lounge room towards the kitchen to look for them. I prayed they would be on the counter and not with her things somewhere.

My phone light skittered around the room as I scanned. My shoulders sagged when I realized they weren't in here, after all.

I decided to try searching her handbag instead, and turned. My heart stopped as two eyes stared back at me and I nearly screamed.

Alex stood there, watching me.

"What are you doing?" he asked.

I let out a breath. *Crap. I can't tell him or he'll tell Savannah.*

"I was getting a glass of water," I replied breathlessly, and he raised an eyebrow at me.

"Why not turn on the light? It's your house."

"I didn't want to wake you," I added quickly, and studied his expression in the dark for signs of scepticism. He nodded slowly.

"What are *you* doing?" I shot back, placing my free hand on my hip.

"The same," he replied coolly. I stepped aside to let him go past, but he didn't move.

Alex was still eyeing me carefully.

"You're going back, aren't you?" he said finally, and I opened my mouth to respond. How did he know?

"Your bag," he added pointedly, before I could fumble another excuse out. Realization came over me, and I shifted the weight of the strap on my shoulder.

"I have to," I said carefully. "Wouldn't you do the same for Savannah if she was back there?"

He considered my words for a moment.

"I guess I would," he replied after a moment. "But how do you intend to get there?"

My cheeks went red with guilt, and I was glad it was dark. He took my silence as not having a plan, and grimaced at me.

"I'll drive you," he said finally, and I was taken aback.

"What? Why?" I pressed, as he crossed the room. He pulled out a stool from the counter, and I spotted a white Prada bag nestled there that was without a doubt Savannah's. I hadn't spotted it in the dark with the stool tucked in. Alex unzipped it and fished out Savannah's car keys.

"Because Savannah would kill me if anything happened to you, and something tells me you'll take a bus if you have to."

I gave him half a sheepish smile and nodded in confirmation. He raised the keys and clasped them in his hand to stop them jingling.

"Let's go, then," he said, waving his hand. He made towards me again, as if heading for the front door, but I stopped him.

"Wait. The back door is quieter," I said, and steered him in the other direction. The two of us slipped out into the night.

CHAPTER TWENTY-ONE

FOREST OF DECEPTION

Ryan's POV

This is crazy*, I thought, as I stood in the chilly night air outside Blakesky's Ziplining Adventures. Under different circumstances, I would have been excited to be here.

Behind me was a tall, wooden fence enclosing the main building where you could get tickets. People trickled in and out, following the path and laughing. Thursday was apparently late-night zip lining, according to Lewis, and they were open until 11PM. It was 9PM now, which was the time she'd chosen. I stared up at the thick pine trees, each one dripping lanterns. Man-made lighting made the forest behind me sparkle as it lined the zip-lining paths.

I turned my attention back to my feet. Last time, it hadn't been so bad, being in a boat with Courtney. Terrifying, but I could swim if she'd tried something. This time, if I tried something, I could fall to my death.

At least we're in public, I thought, shifting uncomfortably on the spot. I was almost certain Courtney would only agree to meeting somewhere private, but she'd surprised me in saying she preferred public. Maybe she felt like we'd be less likely to try something.

"Ryan," came a voice from my left, and a sick feeling developed in my gut. I turned, and there she was. She'd dyed her hair black, and her makeup was heavier than I remembered. But it was her, and you could tell if you looked hard enough.

Her eyes sparkled at the sight of me.

"Ryan," she breathed, and raced over to me. Before I could react, she threw her arms around me. "I knew you'd come around—"

"Get off me," I snarled shortly, and she stepped back in confusion. "I'm here to talk and nothing more. Got it?"

She frowned at me, and I remembered the plan. This was a date to her—and I had to make it feel like one. I had to keep her distracted long enough for the cops to show.

"I mean—let's just take things one step at a time," I added quickly. "I don't want to rush it."

She nodded understandingly. Her top was red, and she wore a black leather jacket and jeans. It seemed fashionable, and *normal*…I wondered where she'd gotten the clothes. Or where she'd been these past seven months, for that matter.

"Before we do anything else, have you got what we agreed on?" I asked.

She reluctantly pulled out a slip of folded paper from her jacket pocket. Her mother's address for Lewis. The agreement of our date was that she'd give it to us.

I took it and slipped it into my jeans pocket.

"Let's go inside, then," she suggested, smiling at me. I bit back a long sigh and nodded stiffly, walking alongside her.

The main building was a small log cabin with a rustic front desk and a lot of posters on the walls promoting the ziplining. A brochure stand stood to the left, and potted plants dotted the small shop.

There was silence between us as we got our tickets. I picked one of the shorter paths, closest to the front entrance, and made a mental note to text Lewis the details as soon as I could. Courtney simply appeared charmed that I'd paid for her ticket, beaming at me.

As we were stepping out of the ticket building—this time through the back entrance—I scanned the area for a toilet block. Different pathways ventured off to different zipline paths, with the tree-lighting appearing as if the forest were filled with fairy lights before our eyes.

Following the signage, I eventually spotted a toilet sign, and turned to Courtney. But she spoke before I could.

"Where's Aubany?"

I swallowed hard, grateful that I'd sent her away this morning.

"She's gone," I replied. "For good."

She smiled again, and I felt a pinch of annoyance.

"It's about time," she replied. "I told you we were meant to be together."

I grimaced back. It was the best I could manage with the anger bubbling inside of me.

"I'll be right back. I need to use the toilet," I told her. It took all of my resolve not to turn around and walk out in that moment. Instead, I kept my movements calm until I reached the bathroom. Once I was out of her sight, I let my expression drop and all my anger showed on my face.

Quickly, I texted Lewis about which path we'd be on, and took a moment to compose myself. I stared in the bathroom mirror as people bustled around me. My hair was slightly messed up from the wind, and my eyes were stony. I felt frozen in place.

This is for her, I thought. *And me—after tonight, we'll both be free of her for good.*

My phone beeped, and Lewis had texted back asking about the address. I told him I had it, and he asked me to take a picture and send it to him. So I pulled out the paper and unfolded it, then snapped a picture in the light. I texted it back, and he seemed satisfied.

Taking a deep breath, I headed back out of the bathroom. Courtney was waiting patiently, leaning against a railing near where the paths veered off. She blended in as a normal person so easily, it was no *wonder* the police hadn't found her after all this time. She even seemed pretty with her hair slightly curled. Too bad I knew better.

She looked up as I made my way back to her.

"Ready?" she asked, her eyes lighting up. She grabbed my hand, and I let her despite the way it made my skin crawl. She had all the enthusiasm and excitement I'd seen in Aubany the first time we went diving together. With Courtney, it seemed to come naturally—like adventure was part of her personality, the way it was part of mine. Unlike Aubany, she didn't need to be convinced.

But that also meant she was reckless, and spontaneous. Part of the fun with Aubany was opening up her worldview to such things, and her grounded nature added balance to our relationship.

Courtney led me to our ziplining path, where a long line already waited. It took time to secure the safety clips, and some people kept hesitating due to the height, which meant it took longer for the line to move along.

All of that was fine by me—the sooner the cops found us, the better.

I didn't have much to say to Courtney, but there were a couple of questions on my mind. I had no idea how she'd react to them, but the constant silence between us was just as awkward. Especially with the way she kept looking at me longingly, waiting for me to speak.

Most people would take it as a sign of disinterest. A bad first date. They'd never call again. But I knew Courtney didn't read signs like that. She'd be back again and again.

"Where have you been all these months?" I asked Courtney finally. She gave me a sly smile.

"That's a secret," she replied.

"Come on, you can trust me," I replied, as convincingly as I could. I forced myself to move closer to her. "I came here with you, didn't I?"

She studied me for a moment.

"Ask me a different question," she said finally. I struggled to think of something worth asking, but there had already been one on my mind. One she likely wouldn't like.

"Why do you hate Aubany so much?"

She frowned at me, which confirmed my suspicions.

"She stole you from me," she replied.

"She didn't," I replied back, and the line moved forward. We shuffled along with it. "I knew Aubany before I knew you. I chose Aubany… *first.*" The last word came out forced.

"She wasn't supposed to be there," Courtney re-plied, folding her arms. "I did all that work to get out of the institution...all that work to set up your trip…I was going to meet you there. But *she* was there, and I hadn't planned for that. She was always there! Just like she was the first time I saw you."

My mind began to race.

"Wait--what?" I replied, shaking my head. "What do you mean you *planned* it?"

"The trip!" she insisted, her brow furrowed as she stared at me like I was an idiot. "We created a fake agency name and gifted your parents the vouchers in the mail so they'd book a holiday there. I waited until the day you were meant to arrive, but Aubany was with you. I never had a chance to get you alone."

What. The. *Fuck?*

All sound around me seemed to drown out as I stepped back from her, processing. She'd been be-hind even *that*. Just how much of this had been planned? How long had she been planning it? What else was she still planning?

"You and Lewis?" I pressed, trying to clarify her words.

A shadow crossed her face.

"Lewis didn't help me. He wanted me to stay in that place. But he doesn't know what it was like to be in there."

If Lewis didn't help her, who did?

Her mother, maybe, I thought. After all, Lewis believed she was alive. How would Courtney know that unless she was working with her? And who else would have the power to get her out of there?

But I remembered the papers saying she'd escaped. Something didn't add up here.

"Why me?" I asked, my throat dry. We were almost at the front of the line now. Her gaze softened.

"Because from the moment I first met you, I knew you were special," she replied. "I never forgot your face. I hoped I'd seen you again...why is it such a bad thing that I wanted to know you better? Even as kids, I never forgot you."

I didn't have enough time to creeped out by her words. The last couple in front of us kicked off, and the staff began hooking up the next kit for us to use.

"First time zip-lining?" the female worker asked, and I nodded. She began reaching around to strap me into the harness firmly. She began explaining all the ropes and clasps, warning me about what not to touch.

"When you get to the bottom, there will be a platform. The staff will guide you on how to disconnect safely. You'll be fine—remember to have fun!"

I nodded again. My head was spinning too much to do more than that. Courtney was behind me as it was a couple's zip-line, also being strapped in.

The sound of sirens hit my ears all of a sudden, and the night sky lit up with red and blue. I felt Courtney stiffen behind me.

"No," she whispered. I tried to turn my head, but I couldn't see her at all the way I was secured. But I felt the moment her panic seized her. She snapped, kicking off hard, and my heart lurched as the staff cried out.

I didn't know if we were secured properly or not, but I clung to the rope for dear life as my feet left the platform. Suddenly we were flying, and I was all alone with her.

"Did you do this?" she screeched at me over the sound of the roaring wind. My heart was pounding as we flew through the golden lights among the trees.

"Answer me!" she demanded. Would the cops follow us? Would they find us at the bottom?

"Yes!" I yelled back.

"Why would you do that to me?" she cried, and I felt a stab of pain as I remembered Aubany's same words from last night.

"Because you need help, Courtney!" I demanded back. "I'm trying to help you! And so is Lewis! You need to understand that there is no *us!*"

Within minutes, we were at the end of the line, skidding onto the platform. Courtney immediately unbuckled herself without waiting for the staff and bolted.

Crap!

I fumbled to get myself free, the staff's hands all over me trying to help, and rushed after her.

Which way did she go?

I scanned, and spotted her red top among the small crowd. Sprinting after her, I pulled out my phone and dialled Lewis.

"What's happening?" he answered.

"She heard the cops and bolted. We're at the other end of the zip line now," I said.

I heard him swear on the other end.

"Don't let her get away! Stay on the phone with me," he insisted as my footsteps thudded after her. She raced between two buildings and straight into the forest. I leapt over a rock, following right behind her.

"Courtney!" I bellowed, but she didn't even stop for me. She zigged and zagged between the trees in the dark, trying to lose me. I kept my eyes narrowed and sharp, trying not to run straight into a tree myself.

She was faster than I expected. After a while, exhaustion caught up with me and I had to stop and catch my breath. I huffed, leaning against a tree.

"Ryan? Ryan, are you still there?" came Lewis' voice from the phone. I raised it to my lips.

"Yeah," I huffed. "But I lost her. She's too quick."

Lewis swore again.

"Dammit. Fine…just come back here. We'll re-group and think of something."

The phone call ended. I was deep in the forest now, with no real sense of which way was which. The faint lights behind me was the only thing I had to guide me back to the ziplining place, but maybe I could still find Courtney.

I began to walk forward, as quietly as I could, keeping my eyes and ears alert. I even turned off my phone.

After ten minutes of walking, the forest began to clear, and I found myself at the edge of the lake. The shore was muddy, and I noticed a strange mark a few yards to my left.

Walking closer, I realized the mud had shifted, leaving an indent like something had been here. A boat, I realized, though it would have been a small one.

Had Courtney escaped on a boat? Had she left it here the entire time as a precaution, in case she needed to make a quick getaway? It seemed very Courtney, and I kicked the muddy shore in frustration.

What were we going to do now? Go another seven months until she made her next move? Would she go after Aubany again?

I have to get back to the others, I decided, and headed towards lights shining out of the trees in the distance.

CHAPTER TWENTY-TWO

THE GREAT ESCAPE

Aubany's POV

I felt the car slow and heard the sound of gravel, which woke me from my sleep. Headlines shone through the trees, illuminating the driveway leading back to Lewis' cabin. We'd arrived.

I noticed the lights were on inside, and Lewis' truck was parked out the front. Alex pulled up behind it, effectively blocking it in at the same time, and cut the engine.

I climbed out, feeling the ache of my legs fade as I stretched them. Alex and I shared a look before approaching the front door. I debated whether to knock or just walk inside, but Alex pushed the door open before I had the chance to do either.

We spotted Melissa and Lewis standing in the living room, and they both turned to us immediately. Horror crossed Melissa's face.

"Aubany? What are you doing back here?" she cried. "You shouldn't be here—"

"Well, I am," I replied shortly, folding my arms. Alex closed the door behind us. "Where's Ryan?"

"He's not back yet," Lewis said, frowning. "We thought that was him pulling up."

"What do you mean he's not back yet?" I asked. "Back from what?"

"Back from…trying to trap Courtney," Melissa admitted slowly. My eyes nearly bulged out of my head.

"What?" I screeched. I demanded that they explain everything, and they did—about how he and Lewis devised a plan to meet with Courtney. In exchange for setting up their meeting, Courtney would

reveal the location of his mother. The cops were meant to trap her, but she'd escaped.

"So, the last you heard from him, he was in the forest with Courtney?" I pressed. Lewis nodded, and my nostrils flared. "Don't you realize what happened last time? She took him away in a boat! This is setting up for the *exact* same thing to happen!"

"We'll find him," Melissa promised, but I was angry with her. I was angry with *all* of them!

"I'm going to find him," I said, turning towards the door again.

"Wait!" Lewis said. "We'll come. But if he's in the forest, that's near the lake. And I know a faster way to get there."

He gestured for us to follow him, and headed for the stairs. Melissa followed, but I hesitated. Why was he leading us upstairs?

He turned his head and noticed I hadn't moved from the door.

"Aubany, come on. You can trust me."

I narrowed my gaze at him, but forced my feet to move as I followed them up the stairs.

Lewis walked the length of the landing all the way to the closed-off bedroom. He opened it, and switched on the light.

I waited in the doorway, watching as he crossed the room and lifted up the heavy, woven rug covering the floor. Dragging it aside, it revealed a trap door.

My eyes widened. I'd been *right!* Courtney *had* been coming and going through this room—except I'd never thought about there being a trap door!

He looked up at me.

"It came with the house and leads to the bottom of the lake—I imagine it was used by previous owners as an escape tunnel? I'm not entirely sure myself..."

Melissa and I exchanged an impressed look. Lewis grabbed the iron handle, which popped out from a groove, and tugged upward. The door creaked open, revealing a ladder that led down into darkness.

"You'll need a torch," Lewis said, crossing to the dresser and opening the top drawer. He grabbed one and passed it over to Melissa, who tested it with two clicks.

"I'll lead you through it myself," Lewis said, and prepared to climb down. But at that moment, the sound of the front door creaking open made us all stop in our tracks.

"Ryan?" Lewis called out, straightening up. I jolted upward with hope.

"Unfortunately not," a voice drawled back loudly from the foyer, and horror seeped through me at the familiar sound.

Lewis' eyes widened, and he immediately pushed the bedroom door so it was only slightly ajar and concealed us from sight.

Courtney was here. I didn't even remember my last encounter with her because she'd knocked me out. I involuntarily began to shake.

"Quick—go now, before she sees you," Lewis whispered to us, but his eyes were locked on me. "I'll stall her and try to find out more about Ryan."

Melissa quickly stepped onto the ladder and began descending. I heard footsteps on the stairs as I went next, and Alex followed after. Lewis shut the trap door after us, locking us into darkness. But after a moment, Melissa flicked the torch on from beneath us.

I stepped off the last rung of the ladder, feeling solid ground beneath me. We were in a cave, which sloped downwards towards the lake—providing what Lewis had said was correct, that is.

"Come on—we don't want to risk her following and finding us," Melissa said, and urged us all to move. The cave was cold and smelt damp and mouldy as we followed the path.

We walked in silence for a while—the only other sound being our footsteps—before Melissa finally spoke.

"Aubany, I want you to know something..."

I didn't answer, but I didn't stop her, either.

"You're my best friend and I'd never do anything to hurt you. The night after Lewis and I fought, he told me the truth about Courtney. I found out the same day as you, just not in the same way. But he explained how he was trying to help her *and* keep her from hurting you. That's why I took his side."

I spared her a glare in response, and she sighed.

"I know I should have told you, and I should have made an effort to support you. But it felt like the right thing at the time, because he clearly knew more about Courtney than I did. I thought I could help you in that way."

I considered her words, then nodded.

"Okay. I understand why you did it," I said carefully, but I wasn't quite ready to forgive her yet. She knew me, though, and she knew she'd made the first step in the right direction. The awkwardness eased between us.

"Do you think Lewis is okay back there?" I asked finally. She shrugged.

"I hope so. But it's his sister. Well...half-sister. I don't think she'd hurt him, by the sound of what he's told me."

What if she hurt Ryan? What if he's bleeding to death out in the woods somewhere?

The thought made me speed up in my tracks as we walked.

Eventually, we made it to the bottom of the sloping cave, only to find a huge boulder blocking the exit. I let out a frustrated groan.

"You've got to be kidding," I mumbled, and pulled out my phone. It lit up, but there was no reception. Plus, I'd forgotten to charge it before I left home, so it was nearly flat.

We all scanned the space, surprised to find it cluttered with various bits and pieces. Much like the underside of the cabin, it was filled with old paddles, boxes, and junk. I wondered if Courtney had been living here. Or maybe she'd been using it as a storage space.

"Maybe I can push the boulder," Alex offered finally, moving closer to inspect it. "At least enough for you both to slip through. I can head back up the tunnel and go back through the trap door. And if not, you'll know where I am, anyway."

There was a small gap already letting moonlight in from the way it was sitting, and Alex placed his hands against it. He began to push, grunting, and his face turned red. I was about to tell him to stop when the boulder moved—just enough for one of us to slip through. Melissa was closer, and she seized the opportunity, leaping through the gap.

At that moment, Alex let out a cry and stepped back, yanking his hand to his chest to cradle it. The boulder rolled back in place, trapping us again.

"Are you okay?" I cried, rushing forward.

"Yeah," he breathed, and carefully flexed his hand, wincing. "I think I just sprained my wrist, is all. I'll try again—"

"No! What if you hurt yourself further?" I insisted, and steered him away from the boulder. With more space, I was able to peer through the gap and see Melissa on the other side—right next to the lake.

"Melissa—you have to go get help. And find Ryan!" I told her through the gap. "Don't worry about us! We'll wait here."

"Are you sure?" she asked, frowning back at me. "Maybe if Alex and I both tried pushing the boulder together...."

I shook my head.

"Just hurry and find Ryan, okay?"

She studied me for a moment, then nodded.

"Okay. I won't be long—I promise!"

With that, she hurried off out of sight, and I was alone with Alex in the cave. In the darkness, I shivered as I heard her footsteps fade away.

I stepped back and exchanged a look with Alex, grimacing.

"Well, maybe there's something else in here that can help us while we wait?" I suggested. I scanned the space again, this time paying more attention to what was down here. Aside from the boxes and paddles, there were rations and blankets too. It definitely seemed like Courtney's hideout-away-from-home.

"Check over there," Alex indicated, pointing with his good hand. "I'll search over here."

I turned and walked across the cave, my back to him. Crouching down, I peered in the darkness at the various boxes, carefully pulling the lids back to search them. I was wary of what I might find, and it was hard to see.

After a moment of inspecting the box, which had nothing but old papers and a half-eaten packet of nuts, I shook my head and turned.

"Nothing over here—"

My eyes widened. The last thing I saw was the paddle Alex swung at me. I felt pain as it hit the side of my head, and then everything went black.

CHAPTER TWENTY-THREE

CRUEL INTENTIONS

Aubany's POV

I remember drifting in and out of consciousness.

The first time, all I saw were the stars swaying above me. I felt a rocking sensation all around me, and by the time I realized I was in a boat, Alex was peering down at me with a hard glare. Then the darkness took me again.

The second time, I heard voices, and felt as if I were being dragged. But pain still throbbed in my head, making my vision blurry, and it was easier to close my eyes and let the pain slip away.

The third time, however, it was like flicking a switch. One second, I was asleep, and with a gasp I snapped awake with a sudden alertness.

I tried to move and looked around, only to find myself bound by my hands and feet in the corner of what looked to be an abandoned shack.

Standing in front of me were Alex and Courtney, which sent a jolt through my body. A part of me still wasn't believing and comprehending the sight. But I couldn't forget the way Alex had hit me with such intention.

This was no coincidence.

Courtney wore a furious gaze, but there was a hint of triumph in her eyes as I struggled against the rope bindings. She folded her arms and practically beamed down at me. Alex, too, looked smug. It was unsettling.

"I wasn't expecting this," were the first words that came to mind as I stared at him.

"That was the point," Alex replied humourlessly, and I felt as if I'd been punched in the stomach with confirmation. I'd *trusted* him. I'd been alone in a car with him!

"I don't understand," I said weakly, and it was true. At this point, every single person had turned on me in some way. Alex had been the only one not to until now. I'd never been so confused in my life, and I didn't know how I'd trust anybody ever again.

Courtney seemed delighted by an opportunity to brag to me. She stepped forward.

"Alex is my cousin," Courtney explained. "The three of us used to play together when we were kids."

It clicked into place—Alex's grandmother lived in Blakesky. I'd chalked it up to nothing but a coincidence until now...but it made perfect sense.

"When I was taken away to the institution, Alex was the only one who visited me. He spent his pocket money on the bus to come see me. He helped me escape, and he helped me plan the Nula Island vacation for Ryan's family."

Her gaze darkened.

"Then *you* showed up. You weren't meant to be there."

My head began to spin as I listened to her, but she wasn't stopping to let me process.

"I needed to get you away from Ryan—so Alex stepped in and infiltrated the little friend group you were building there to give me intel."

I felt sick. The night Savannah met Alex was the same night we met Courtney. It had been no coincidence that he'd asked to dance with her. Perhaps it had been a miracle they'd clicked so quickly, but *still.*...

"I can't believe this is happening," I breathed, and Courtney laughed at my reaction. I'd *never* suspected Alex, or seen any of this coming!

"When things didn't go to plan, I spent months trying to figure out a way to separate the two of you.

I needed to get you someplace alone. So I coaxed Lewis into helping me. But it seems he's sided with you, too."

She gave me a long, hard look.

"For some reason, everyone always chooses you. Ever since I was young, I had to fight for what I wanted, but you're just given it. You have Ryan. You have everyone protecting you. And you manage to derail my plans time and time again. It seems that you're always in the way, and I'm tired of it. As long as you live, you have a hold over Ryan's heart."

She crossed the room to a table behind them, and grabbed something, before adding,

"But that changes today."

A knife glinted in the light of a lantern sitting there, and my breath hitched as I remembered the pain last time.

Not again--please, not again!

I had to stall her—Ryan would find me, wouldn't he? Or Melissa would, at least. She would be looking for Alex and I. But where *were* we, exactly?

"I can't believe you did all of this over Ryan!" I said shakily, trying to keep myself from screaming in hysterics as she approached me with the knife. The razor-sharp edge taunted me. "How long have you been planning all of this?"

"It doesn't matter," she said, stepping closer.

"Wait!" I begged, shrinking as far against the wall as I could. "Please...Ryan and I aren't even together anymore. I'm no threat to you."

"I was with him tonight, and he *still* talks about you," she said menacingly. "You can tell he still cares, and the only way to eliminate any hope that he might get you back is for you to disappear for good."

Tears began to well in my eyes. She was decided, and *crazy,* and it was useless trying to reason with her. I began to shake, watching the blade with wide eyes.

"Courtney, I'm begging you..." I whispered. "Just let me talk to him one last time. If you're going to kill me...let me call him."

She considered my words, studying me intently. I kept my expression neutral, trying not to show my fear and desperation.

"Please…let me say goodbye."

CHAPTER TWENTY-FOUR

THE FINAL BLOW

Ryan's POV

It took an hour for me to arrive back at the cabin after I'd walked through the forest and left Blakesky Ziplining Adventures—which had been crawling with cops questioning everyone and had delayed my exit.

I checked my phone again as I walked up the gravel to find six missed calls from Lewis, and two from Melissa. They were probably just wondering where I was.

I looked to my left as I walked. Only Lewis' truck was parked outside, as expected.

Heading up the small front steps, I pushed the cabin door open and entered. All the lights were on, but it appeared empty. A fire was still lit in the fire-place, but it had died to embers. I thought it was un-usual that they hadn't put the fire out.

"Lewis?" I called, scanning the space. I heard footsteps from upstairs, and Melissa emerged on the landing.

"Ryan!" she cried, and raced along the landing towards the stairs. "Oh my gosh, I'm *so* happy to see you!"

Wow. That was a first.

"Have you seen Lewis?" she asked me as she de-scended quickly. I frowned.

"No, I haven't. I just got back from the zip-lining. The cops were everywhere—"

"Oh, shit," Melissa breathed, her face going pale, as she bought a hand to cover her mouth. "What if she *did* hurt him?"

"Who?" I pressed.

"Courtney. She was here," Melissa said. Only at that moment, as she moved more into the light, did I notice the twigs in her hair. Like she'd been running through the forest herself. "She came here, so we all rushed into this secret tunnel that's upstairs and Lewis stayed behind to stall her."

I shook my head, trying to follow.

"Who else was here apart from you and Lewis?"

"Aubany. She came back with Alex."

Panic crashed through me instantly. She was *here?* With Courtney on the loose and clearly *pissed* at us?

"You have to tell me everything," I insisted, but Melissa shook her head, tears in her eyes.

"There's no time—Aubany and Alex are trapped in the cave where the tunnel leads out. And Lewis and Courtney aren't here. What if they went down the tunnel, too, and now Aubany and Alex can't get out?"

Why the hell were we still standing here?

I rushed past her towards the stairs.

"Show me," I said, and we both raced back up to the landing. But before I could take another step, my phone rang again.

I pulled it out and looked down. The caller ID said Aubany, and my heart leapt.

"Aubany?" I cried, answering it. I only heard breathing on the other end at first, so I repeated myself. Melissa was watching with wide eyes.

"Ryan," came a sniffle. Relief swept through me at the sound of her voice.

"Aubs, are you okay?" I asked. "Where are you?"

"I don't know," she said in a small voice. The connection crackled slightly, like there was poor reception on the other end. "But I wanted to hear your voice one last time."

Her voice had a whine to it, like she was clearly crying…or trying her best not to. Another sniffle.

"What are you talking about?" I asked, my heart pounding wildly as I paced the landing. "What's happened?"

"What's happening?" Melissa whispered, but I ignored her.

"That's enough," came another voice, but it was faint. Aubany let out a ragged sob.

"Ryan, I love you," she blurted out quickly. "And I'm sorry—"

There was a clattering sound on the other end, and I strained to hear what was happening.

"Aubs?" I cried. My free hand gripped the landing railing as I tried to listen. My knuckles started to turn white.

"Please..." came her voice, but it sounded far away now. She was clearly sobbing hard between her words. I'd never heard her more scared and distraught.

"Aubany!" I yelled down the line. But it was useless. I didn't know where she was. I couldn't reach her.

I *never* should have sent her back alone. I should have stayed with her.

"Please don't hurt me!" she sobbed, and all I could do was listen, a sick feeling developing in my stomach. The sobbing got louder. "Oh, my God, no. Ryan--*Ryan!"* she shrieked desperately. There was a strangled scream, followed by a loud smash.

Then the phone line went dead. I listened to the monotone dial sound, staring wide eyed into nothingness, the sound ringing in my ears. My phone slipped from my grasp, falling to the floor with a clatter I barely noticed.

EPILOGUE

Ryan's POV

It had been six weeks since Aubany's final phone call to me.

I stood in the hallway at school, staring at her locker as people passed me. I had more classes…college applications to look over…and the bell for third period had already rung. But I couldn't seem to move my feet, because none of it seemed to matter anymore.

I didn't have to guess at what had happened, because along with Aubany, Lewis had never returned either. I wish I'd never trusted him, and I was almost certain he had something to do with it. If I ever saw him again—

"Hey," came a voice on my right. I glanced absently, and saw Melissa standing there. She had dark circles under her eyes, like she hadn't been sleeping well. "Come on. I'll walk you to class."

I didn't respond, turning my attention back to the locker. Melissa let out a small sigh.

"I miss her too, Ryan," she said quietly. "But we don't know if she's really dead. The police are still looking for a body."

"They won't find a body," I said blandly. "If they couldn't find Courtney for seven months, they won't find anything she doesn't want found. Including Aubany."

"Well, Savannah thinks—"

I turned and began walking away. I didn't want to hear any more. I'd heard enough when my Mom had come to get me from Blakesky and bought me home. I'd watched as Aubany's parents stood out in front of their house and screamed at me, blaming me for their daughter's reckless actions.

I'd looked Savannah in the eye as she stood with them, and her accusing gaze had been more than enough to tell me what they now thought of me.

I had once thought of them as friends and family. Now they hated me because Aubany had loved me so much, she put herself in danger for it.

Didn't they understand what it was like to go on living, *knowing* that, when I, too, had loved her so deeply?

"Ryan, wait," Melissa said, grabbing my shoulder as she caught up to me. I slumped my shoulders, but made myself face her.

"I know we haven't gotten along in the past, but I was there when it happened. You're not the only one suffering through this. But I'm choosing to believe she's still alive. After all, there's no solid evidence. When they found Alex unconscious in the forest, he had no recollection of what happened. She could have run, for all we know!"

They'd found Alex near where the cave let out. He'd since gone back home to Miami.

I sighed.

I didn't want false hope. I wanted answers, and I wanted justice. All I'd ever tried to do was protect her. And knowing that Courtney had weaved a bigger web than we initially knew unnerved me. She'd never truly been safe from her...but maybe she would have been if I hadn't fallen in love with her.

At least then, Courtney wouldn't have had a reason to target her.

"Just go to class, Melissa," I muttered. The hallways were emptying fast, and the second bell would ring any minute.

Melissa hesitated, then rolled her eyes at me and stalked off on her own. Even though she'd been trying to be nice to me lately, you could tell it was a struggle at times.

It would be better if she didn't bother. Her best friend wouldn't be dead if I had left Aubany alone to begin with.

With a sigh, I reached my own locker and unlocked it. It swung open, and I reached in for a book—only to then notice a folded piece of paper tucked inside the locker.

Frowning, I plucked the paper from the shelf and unfolded it. It was only then that I remembered what it was—the piece of paper Courtney had given me with her mother's location. I stared at it for a moment, and wondered what I might find there.

What if Lewis was there?

The thought of seeing him again, and confronting him about what had happened...it gave me resolve.

For the first time in weeks, I felt motivated. Maybe I'd get the answers I sought after all.

I turned towards the school exit, my grip tightening on the piece of paper, and slammed the locker door shut.

IS AUBANY DEAD OR ALIVE?

join my Patreon to access my exclusive

membership community and **get a clue.**

VISIT: https://www.patreon.com/join/psmalcolm

book three coming soon

ACKNOWLEDGEMENTS

Another book, another acknowledgements page.

There are a lot of people who have reached out to me over the years expressing how much they loved the first Ryan Rupert book. For some, it was a book they couldn't put down when they're not even a big fan of reading. For others, it's become their favourite book.

These comments mean the absolute world to me, knowing that SOVWRR was the first book I ever wrote that I considered good enough to publish, the first book I ever released, and the first book I ever published entirely by myself.

My biggest fear with this book was that it wouldn't do the first book justice. As I've grown over the years in maturity, I feel that my characters have too. Maintaining their original humour and chemistry was a challenge.

So, I want to especially thank the fans of the first book in this sequel, and I hope with all my heart this book was just an enjoyable. Without you, this book wouldn't exist because I wouldn't have had the motivation to complete this series. You guys know who you are.

(P.S: Sorry for the major cliff-hanger. See you in book three! *wink*)

ABOUT THE AUTHOR

P.S.Malcolm is the author of the *Starlight Chronicles Series* and the *Ryan Rupert Series*. She is a tea enthusiast, cat lover, and floral fanatic with a deep passion for writing stories.

She grew up in the tropics of Australia, close to the beach and surrounded by the bush.

Her other works, personal endeavors, and social media links can be found on her website: psmalcolm.com